Becoming Keeper

Also by Suneé le Roux

The Reverie Flash Fiction Series

A Spark of Reverie
A Flight of Reverie

Standalone Short Stories

Spirit Caller

The Mythical Menagerie Series

Keeper of Exotic Animals
Becoming Keeper

Myth Hunter
Myth Keeper

Becoming Keeper

MYTHICAL MENAGERIE PREQUEL

Suneé le Roux

Strawberry Moon Press

ISBN (Paperback): 978-0-7961-3522-3

Author's Note

Although this prequel can be read as a standalone story, it would make more sense if you've read the first two volumes of the Mythical Menagerie series, Myth Hunter and Myth Keeper, first. The events in this novel take place before these two books, which is why it classifies as a prequel, but there might be some Easter eggs in this story that will be more fun to discover if you're already familiar with the main character.

However, if you choose to read this story first, I hope you'll enjoy it and be intrigued enough to continue with the rest of the series!

This novel makes use of UK English spelling and syntax.

Table of Contents

Becoming Keeper..1

Bonus Flash Fiction....................................79

- Bottenfeldt's Disappointment.............81
- In Need of a Fishbowl.........................84
- A Flag to Capture................................88
- Better on Our Side...............................92

Acknowledgements.....................................97

Want More?..98

Please Review..100

About the Author.......................................101

Becoming Keeper

Amari stared thoughtfully at the deer grazing on the dew-drenched grass of the Grove, her hands fidgeting with the leopard print scarf around her neck. Although this was her third year at Oxford, she still wasn't used to the crispness of these English summer mornings, or the pale blue sky that could turn to a soft drizzle at a moment's notice. Behind her, the Gothic façade of Magdalen College reminded her she was a long way from home.

One of the younger deer stopped to sniff the air and turned its head towards her. Amari dug into her satchel, pulling out a slice of bread she'd saved from breakfast, and leaned against the railing, hoping the fawn would come closer. In their video calls, her brothers at home often teased her when she told them about her morning commune with the deer, but to her it was a lifeline that kept the homesickness at bay.

The deer stared at her for a few moments, and then it moved closer. It eyed her nervously, until desire won out, and it started nibbling on the bread in her hand. Amari smiled. She reached out her other hand and gently stroked the soft fur on the fawn's head. It had a white diamond-shaped patch just between its ears. It ignored her as it continued nipping eagerly at the bread.

Suddenly, Amari's mobile buzzed and the deer's head jerked up, startled. It darted away as Amari sighed. She pulled the phone out of her pocket and glanced at the screen. A reminder to go work on her paper.

Her shoulders slumped. With most of her final exams behind her, the only real hurdle still standing between her and that all-important piece of official paper was one final essay she'd been putting off for weeks now. It was due in four days and she still hadn't written a word.

Her phone buzzed again, and she looked at the text message that popped up. It was from Doctor Clarke, her zoology supervisor.

-- *Come, if you have a moment. I'm about to test the next iteration…* --

Amari hesitated. Zoology was an elective, an extra subject she'd taken for personal interest only. It didn't count towards her final marks, and it definitely wouldn't contribute towards the philosophy paper she had to write. The smart thing would be to excuse herself and head straight for the library, not the lab.

But the lab was the easier option.

She swiped the reminder away. She still had some time.

Amari tossed the last bits of crumbs onto the grass and hitched her satchel over her shoulder. Waving goodbye to the deer, she headed towards the Science Area campus.

※※※

Amari peered through the small window set into the door of Lab C, where she could see Doctor Clarke hunched over something on a table at the back. Amari knocked on the door and the woman beckoned her to come in without looking up.

The rubber soles of her sneakers squeaked as she walked through the pristine white room and

Doctor Clarke finally lifted her head. Her pale blonde hair shone in the bright fluorescent light, and the designer pants suit and expensive jewellery dangling from around her neck and wrists couldn't be more at odds with the sterile environment. She looked like she should be in a boardroom somewhere, presenting graphs showing upward financial trends, but Amari knew that behind Doctor Clarke's flashy exterior lurked a keen scientific mind and an unquenchable thirst for knowledge.

"Ah, there you are!" her supervisor exclaimed. "I'm about to inject Specimen 23-A with Version 73.104. Hold it down for me, please! It keeps squirming, and I want to see how it reacts to the serum while it's still alive."

Amari saw a little brownish mouse cowering in a small cage on the lab table. She dropped her satchel on the floor before opening the cage's lid as the doctor pulled on a pair of blue latex gloves. The mouse looked up at Amari with fright-filled eyes nearly as large as its round ears.

"Ow," she said, wincing as she picked it up with both hands. "It's spiky."

Doctor Clarke nodded as she pulled a container filled with a viscous liquid that looked like molten quicksilver closer. "It's an African Spiny," she said as she pulled the liquid into a long-needled syringe. "Amazing little critters. They can regrow skin and cartilage without leaving any scars. I'm hoping this one's regenerative genes will be the catalyst the serum needs."

"What happened to the planarian?" Amari asked as Doctor Clarke brought the needle closer. The little mouse's heart hammered against Amari's palm, and she couldn't help but feel sorry for it. Previous iterations of the serum hadn't reacted well with the flatworms the doctor had been experimenting on. Amari hoped the mouse wasn't about to fizzle into a brownish goo, too.

Doctor Clarke snorted. "Worms weren't getting me anywhere. It was time to start testing with mammals. Hold it still. One, two."

The mouse tensed into a little ball in Amari's hands as the needle pierced its skin. Doctor Clarke pressed the plunger, steady and efficiently injecting the serum into the small body. Amari held her breath as the mouse lay quivering in her hands.

Doctor Clarke peered at the creature, her mouth pressed into a thin line. Suddenly, her eyes widened and her mouth formed a surprised oh.

Amari yelped as she dropped the mouse into the cage again, staring at the bubble of blood forming in her palm where a thin white line stood out against her brown skin. Her eyes darted towards the mouse and she gasped as the bristly hair on its back turned into razor-sharp blades.

"What the –" she said, swallowing the expletive as the mouse turned to look at her with blood-red eyes. It growled, and if Amari hadn't been looking straight at it, she would have sworn she was hearing a lioness warning another predator away from a kill.

Doctor Clarke darted forward and snapped the lid of the cage down, the lock clicking into place just as the mouse lunged at Amari. It hit the steel wire with such force it nearly knocked the cage off the table. Amari jumped backwards, swearing. Her gaze shot towards her supervisor. Doctor Clarke was staring intently at the mouse.

"What have you done?" Amari gaped at the rampaging animal as it dashed itself against the walls of the cage again and again until the bars were spattered crimson. "Make it stop!"

"I don't have to," Doctor Clarke said grimly. She pointed at the cage and Amari saw the mouse slump into a corner. Its body shook for a moment, and then it lay still. Carefully, Amari took a step closer until she could see the mouse's tongue lolling out, its red eyes staring sightlessly at nothing.

"It's dead." Amari's hands trembled, remembering the pounding heartbeat she'd felt just moments before. This was nothing like the worms. Warm tears pricked at the corners of her eyes.

"It's just a mouse, Amari," Doctor Clarke said callously. She picked up a pencil from where it was laying on top of her notebook and prodded the little body. "Not quite the effect I'd anticipated, but maybe the physical transformation was the serum's reaction with the mouse's innate protective genes? Oh! Here." The woman pressed a disinfectant wipe into Amari's injured hand.

Amari wiped the blood from her palm, carefully flexing her fingers. The cut stung like crazy, but it was small and would heal quickly. It would probably make writing a little difficult, though. The thought sent a spike of anxiety down her spine and also reminded her she'd procrastinated long enough.

"I'd better go," she said.

"Mm-hmm." Doctor Clarke was writing frantically in her notebook. Amari knew from experience the woman would be lost in her own thoughts for hours now, running possible variations through the lab's high-tech computer until the next iteration of the serum's formula was ready for testing.

Amari glanced at the glistening quicksilver liquid, and then at the dead mouse, monstrous in its transformation. She shuddered. Hopefully Doctor Clarke would get it right before another mouse had to suffer.

Hitching her satchel back onto her shoulder,

Amari tiptoed out of the lab, wincing at every squeak her sneakers made. A cloudless sky greeted her outside. For a moment, she was tempted to head towards the River Cherwell, where she knew some of Magdalen's seniors would already be doing some celebratory punting ahead of graduation.

She sighed. She needed to earn her place with them first. There'd be no punting for her at all if she didn't finish this paper. Time enough to have fun when the work was done.

※※※

The silence hanging over the Bodleian Library's reading room felt even more oppressive than usual. A few other students were scattered around the room, anxiously trying to cram as much information in before their final exams. Amari slumped into her chair, chewing on the end of a pencil while she stared out the window at tourists taking pictures of the old building in the fading light.

She could have been one of those people. When she ran home with the news that she'd been granted a scholarship at one of Britain's most prestigious universities, her parents had been excited about her career prospects, but it was the thought of exploring the world that had thrilled her. She hadn't known what she wanted to do with her life back then and would have accepted any course they picked if it meant getting to live abroad for a while. As it turned out, enrolling for Oxford's much-respected Philosophy, Politics and Economics degree had been a mistake.

Amari had hated every minute of it.

She'd maintained her marks just high enough to satisfy her bursary's requirements, but most of her energy went into pursuing extra subjects that interested her more – flitting between classes ranging from biology to horticulture to classical literature. She was the top student in ancient mythology and a close second in zoology, and everyone in her dormitory came to her when they needed help with geography. She'd sat classes for and could get by in half a dozen modern languages and had spent an entire semester delving into the semantics of the more obscure ancient languages.

And she still didn't know what she wanted to be when she grew up.

A bee buzzed past Amari's head, so loud in the hushed stillness that it made her jump. Clicking her tongue in annoyance, she grabbed the leaflet she'd been using as a bookmark and swatted at the insect. It batted up against the closed window, trying to escape, in vain.

Amari knew the feeling. She looked at the leaflet in her hand. Crumbling Urquhart Castle hulked against the cobalt shores of Loch Ness, the verdant Highlands of Scotland in the background. She'd never imagined grass could be that green! Where she'd grown up in Johannesburg, on the South African Highveld, the plains were covered in shades of yellow and olive green. It was hot and dry and beautiful in its own way, but she desperately needed to see that emerald countryside with her own eyes.

But first, she had to write this damn essay.

Shoving the leaflet underneath the stack of books on her desk, Amari contemplated the blank piece of paper in front of her. After hours of research, cross-referencing, and pulling her hair out, she still had nothing to show for it. Professor Harris, her student supervisor and philosophy lecturer, had told the class to write an argumentative essay on any topic related to ethics that interested them. Amari's average for the subject had dipped this semester and Professor Harris had warned her she'd need to write something worthy of an A if she didn't want to repeat the subject next year.

The thought of delaying her graduation by another year scared Amari more than walking alone through the streets of Jo'burg at night did.

The bee buzzed around her head again, and Amari wafted her hand angrily at it. It darted straight at her and landed on her nose. Grunting, she smacked at it and grimaced as she slapped herself in the face. Stunned, the bee landed on the desk, its wings still buzzing annoyingly.

Slowly, Amari reached for the textbook on top of the pile stacked next to her blank notepad. As quick as she could, she slammed the book down on the desk, and swore as the bee buzzed off again, unharmed. Growling, she jumped out of her chair and was about to attack the insect again when someone cleared his throat behind her.

"I think you'd find it less annoying if you help it achieve its intent," a deep voice with a thick German accent said softly.

Amari turned to see Professor Bottenfeldt strolling past her to open the window. The bee buzzed through the gap and disappeared into the deepening orange glow of the setting sun. Smiling benignly, the Professor closed the window again. He turned towards her, his watery blue eyes twinkling with amusement beneath his tweed flat cap. Dressed in a three-piece tweed suit and with his silver beard cropped close to his square jaw, he looked the epitome of an Oxford don.

"All life has value, Amari. Even a little bee like this. Remember its role in the grand tapestry of life."

"It's just a stupid insect," Amari mumbled,

feeling heat rise to her cheeks. "It was distracting me from my paper."

"Was it?" Professor Bottenfeldt lifted an eyebrow as he looked down at her blank notepad. "Industrious little creatures, bees. Always working with a single-minded purpose. It looks to me like you could take some pointers from this stupid little insect, Miss Kerubo."

Amari wished she could escape out the window, too. Of all the lecturers she'd met on campus, Emeritus Professor Jacob Bottenfeldt was her favourite. He'd retired during her first year at Oxford and, although he didn't teach anymore, she still frequently found him in the Bodleian Library continuing his research in mythology, a subject for which they both shared a passion.

She sat down behind the desk again, avoiding his gaze. She couldn't bear the weight of his disapproval.

Professor Bottenfeldt cleared his throat. "I can see you're busy, and I don't want to keep you from your studies. When you have a moment, read this." He dropped a small stack of stapled printouts on the desk. She glanced at the heading of what looked like a research article: *'The Grindylow: Mythical Monster or Maligned Child Minder?'* by James Davids.

Amari rolled her eyes. "Not him again. Any good this time?"

Professor Bottenfeldt chuckled. "Read it and tell me what you think."

Amari's fingers twitched towards the article, but she picked up her pencil instead. "I will. As soon as I finish my own paper. My degree depends on it, unfortunately."

"I'll leave you to it, then," the Professor said. He looked at the pile of books stacked on the desk and grunted. "When you're done with Kant and

Kierkegaard, come find me." He winked at her before strolling off again.

Amari returned her attention to the notepad in front of her. The blank lines stared mutely back at her. She tapped her foot fretfully until she noticed two students glaring at her from across the room. Then she read a passage from one of the books, before sharpening her pencil to a point with which she could have vivisected a flatworm. She stared up at the painted panels of the vaulted ceilings, and then wondered if a cup of tea would help her concentrate.

She was just about to get up in search of a warm beverage when her eyes fell on the research article Professor Bottenfeldt had left behind. Amari scanned the abstract, shaking her head. It looked like Davids was just as delusional as always. Why the academic world kept humouring him was beyond her. Mythical creatures weren't real. Even her gogo, who spent more time in the ancestral spirit plane than the real world, knew that.

"Focus, Amari," she berated herself softly. Was there something she could use here? Could she write about the ethical implications of repeatedly publishing the papers of a so-called academic who'd clearly crossed the bridge dividing fiction from reality? The man's theories were just as hilarious as an elephant drunk on fermented Marula fruit.

His overactive imagination clearly wasn't burdened by writer's block.

She sighed again, her gaze travelling to the window. Outside, the sky was getting dark. Streetlights twinkled like shimmering fairy trails leading towards better pursuits.

Amari surged to her feet, ignoring her conscience as she tossed everything but the library books into her satchel. Tonight was a lost cause. She didn't have any ideas, and without ideas, she wouldn't have any words. And with every second that passed it became ever clearer that she wouldn't find inspiration inside this stuffy room. She needed some fresh air.

Practically sprinting, Amari emerged from the library like a butterfly from a cocoon.

She needed a distraction, and she knew exactly where she would find one.

※※※

The road to distraction led past Hertford College and underneath the Bridge of Sighs. Amari had walked this path a thousand times before, but the goosebumps that lifted on her arms were entirely new. She paused underneath the Gothic structure spanning across New College Lane, suddenly remembering that folklorists considered bridges to be gateways, portals to otherworldly realms. If that were true, she'd be standing at a threshold right now, her goosebumps the result of magic mixing with the mundane.

Intrigued by the idea, she lifted her gaze towards the bottom of the bridge and felt her eyes widen. She'd never noticed the intricate decorations carved into the stone before, looping and twirling like arcane graffiti across the entire span.

Something flickered in the corner of her eyes. Amari turned and gasped as soft ethereal lights floated all around her. The skin on her arms prickled where the lights touched her, and her ears were filled with their murmurs, the sound of lost secrets whispered by a thousand sparkling voices.

She tilted her head, listening intently. She had that nagging feeling that she could almost understand what they were saying, like a forgotten word on the tip of her tongue. One sound was repeated more frequently than the others. It rolled inside Amari's head until she felt dizzy, the lights a swirling maelstrom around her that sent her stumbling out from underneath the bridge.

Suddenly, the otherworldly flickers were gone and her head was clear again.

Amari blinked. She could hear cars hooting in Holywell Street and the only radiance twinkling around her now came from the streetlights sputtering to life overhead. She glanced up at the bridge – it was just an old bridge, nothing magical about it.

"Too many musty old libraries," Amari muttered as she turned her back on it and hurried past the college. She noticed her hands were shaking and she thrust them deep into her jacket's pockets.

She needed a distraction now more than ever. And something to settle her nerves.

※※※

The smell of cheap beer assailed her nose as soon as she walked through the pub door. *The Tenth Muse* was practically throbbing with student conversation and Amari felt the tension fade from her shoulders, her worries – and the strange sounds murmuring at the edge of her consciousness – forgotten for now.

"Amari! Over here!"

She pushed through the crowd towards a booth in the corner at the back where Becca, her next-door neighbour at Magdalen's dorms, waved her eagerly over. Amari slid into the seat opposite her, dropping her satchel to the floor and reaching for the bowl of peanuts in the centre of the sticky table. She popped a few nuts into her mouth, but then paused, her hand still in the air, as she realised Becca was looking at her with that twinkle in her eyes that could only mean she had another hare-brained scheme in the works.

"What?" Amari asked, narrowing her eyes at Becca.

"You don't have an exam tomorrow, do you?" Becca asked sweetly, her eyes scanning the crowd over Amari's shoulder.

"No…"

Becca's face lit up and Amari turned to see a guy heading towards their booth. He put three tankards of beer on the table before taking his place on the bench beside her friend. Becca flashed him a smile as she pulled a pint closer.

"Amari, this is Tristan."

Amari considered the newcomer. He had the classically Scandinavian good looks that defined most of Becca's string of boyfriends, but with a brooding intensity Amari hadn't seen in any of her previous choices before. As he pushed one of the drinks towards her, she noticed a stylised image of the globe tattooed on the inside of his wrist.

Amari took a sip of beer. "PPE," she said. "And you?"

"Not a student," Tristan replied drily, before taking a long swig from his glass. "I prefer action over books."

"Tristan's an *activist*," Becca declared, swooning at him in what Amari could only describe as love-struck admiration. "And he's been in jail. Twice!"

Amari coughed as her beer went down wrong. Her gaze flitted to Tristan, who at least had the good grace to look embarrassed. "Just the holding cells," he said. "That doesn't count."

"It absolutely counts," Becca gushed, and Amari silently agreed with her. "But they won't catch you this time, because this time Amari will be there to help."

Amari spluttered over her beer again. "Excuse

me, what?" she asked.

"Oh, nothing too dangerous!" Becca exclaimed. "Nothing *illegal*." She bent down and whispered loudly: "We just need you to get us into the biology lab after dark."

Amari lifted an eyebrow at her friend. "The biology lab?"

Becca dipped her head at Tristan. "Tell her."

Tristan sat back in his seat, folding his arms across his chest as he studied Amari. "How do I know I can trust her? She looks like she'd squeal on us the moment someone threatened her with a B minus."

Amari huffed indignantly. She'd had plenty of B minuses. Especially this last year.

Becca laughed as if Tristan was wit incarnate. "Don't be silly. *Of course* we can trust her. Besides, as I've said – it's not illegal. *Technically*. Classrooms are at the disposal of students. The fact that we'll be there after hours won't matter because Amari will have unlocked the door for us, which means our access won't be unauthorised. We won't be breaking and entering. Trust me, I'm a law student."

"What do you need from the lab, anyway?" Amari couldn't help but ask.

Tristan eyed her for a few moments longer, and then he leaned forward on his elbows and lowered his voice to a conspiratorial whisper. "We've had a tip-off of an animal smuggling ring operating out of Oxford. I've been in town for a few months now, keeping an eye out for any suspicious activity, and I've noticed a black unmarked van coming and going into Science Area campus, unloading and transferring crates to and from the biology lab."

Amari scoffed. "That could be anything. The lab regularly needs supplies."

Tristan nodded. "True, but why do it at the dead of night when no one else is around?"

Amari shrugged. "There could be many reasons. That doesn't mean anything elicit is happening. Who are 'we', by the way?"

Tristan clenched his chiselled jaw. "The organisation I work for."

"They're like Greenpeace," Becca chimed in cheerfully. "They look after the welfare of animals."

A chill ran down Amari's spine as she remembered the mouse Doctor Clarke had experimented on that morning. That would certainly draw the ire of an animal rights organisation, especially if they'd seen the mutated monster it had turned into. Amari took a swallow of beer to wash away the bitter taste that suddenly filled her mouth. She supported Doctor Clarke's research, but she wasn't so sure about her methods anymore.

But she couldn't jeopardise her future for Becca's latest crush.

"It's too risky," she said, holding up her hands to ward off her friend's protests. "I can't afford to get into trouble. If someone catches us, you'd get a slap on the wrist, but I could have my student visa revoked and be deported."

Tristan frowned at her until Amari wondered if his features would be permanently etched into a scowl. Finally, he nodded. "You don't have to get involved. A key would make things easier, but I know my way around a locked door. Either way, I need to see what's in there." His cold blue eyes bore into her until she almost felt the need to come clean about the neglected goldfish she'd had to flush down the toilet when she was eleven. "Are you in or out?"

Amari's gaze flickered to Becca, who was

scrolling away on her phone like they weren't in the middle of a potentially life-changing discussion. When Amari had first arrived at Magdalen's doors, fresh off the train from Heathrow, it had been Becca who had welcomed her and showed her how to navigate all the simple day-to-day things that locals took for granted but that confounded foreigners like Amari. They'd laughed about Amari's literal pronunciation of her home college's name (she still didn't understand why "Magdalen" should sound like "Maudlin") and bonded after their first late night chip-shop-run. Amari, in an effort to fit in as much as possible for someone with her skin tone, had styled her accent on Becca's clipped upper-class diction and had unwaveringly supported her friend's never-ending list of causes that varied from the eccentric to the downright ridiculous.

But a failed campaign could have far-reaching repercussions this time. For Amari, at least.

"Out." She slammed her empty beer glass on the table and rose to her feet. "Sorry, but I know there's nothing in there but mice. I can't risk my future for that."

Tristan fell back into his seat, his lips pursed into a thin, disapproving line, but Becca glared up at her. "Where's your compassion, Amari? They could be *experimenting* on them!"

Amari shrugged. "They're just mice," she said with a feigned nonchalance that left a sour taste in her mouth.

She slung her satchel over her shoulder and pushed her way through the crowd, her back rigid as she felt their eyes on her. Ignoring the voice in her head that warned her that Becca might get into serious trouble without her help, Amari hurried out of the bar.

※※※

It was dark outside and an unseasonably cold mist bathed the Baroque buildings around Holywell Street in a strangely eerie glow. Amari tucked at her scarf until the chill gave up trying to nip down the back of her neck and wrapped her arms around herself while she considered her next move. For a moment, she was tempted to head back towards the library, but her head felt muffled, like her ears were stuffed with cotton wool. With the din of the pub gone, she realised the strange voices she'd heard underneath the bridge were still there, bouncing around her head like a particularly annoying song stuck on repeat.

She hid a yawn behind the back of her hand. Perhaps it was time to call it a night.

She stepped into the street, intending to cross it, when the sound of a car horn startled her. Two bright lights suddenly flickered into being and Amari froze as they barrelled towards her, like a deer caught in the headlights. The vehicle swerved at the last minute, the wind of its passing buffeting against her. Heart hammering in her chest, Amari stared after it as it turned the corner, almost on two wheels, and switched its lights off again, disappearing into the mist.

A black van. With no licence plates. Heading towards Science Area in the middle of the night.

She deliberated for a moment over whether to go back into the pub and tell Tristan about it, but then decided it would only cast more fuel onto his fire. She wanted to see for herself whether his suspicions were true.

Amari tucked her hands into her jacket and set off in the direction the van had disappeared.

※※※

Although it was late, the gate leading into campus stood wide open. Glancing guiltily at the CCTV camera mounted on the wall, Amari slipped past the gates. Mist roiled about her, clinging damply to her black curls. If it was going to mess up her hair, she hoped it would at least also obscure her features on the security footage.

Amari walked along the path towards the biology labs, her footsteps crunching loudly on gravel in the unnatural silence.

There! A dark shadow loomed out of the mists. It was the unmarked van that had nearly run her over. And it was parked right next to the labs' service entrance, just like Tristan had said.

Swallowing nervously, Amari ventured closer.

There was no one inside the driver's cab. Could there be something in the back? She tried the handle. Locked.

She jumped as voices suddenly filled the silence. Startled, she looked left and right but saw nothing but mist, before realising there was no one around but her. And the voices in her head. Still repeating the same sounds they had whispered underneath the bridge, over and over again.

Amari's lips formed the sounds. She breathed the word out. The lock on the van clicked. The voices fell silent.

Amari's hand shook as she reached towards the handle. Tried it. The door swung open.

Spooked, Amari peered into the back of the van. The hold was dark and she couldn't see anything, but she sensed there was something inside. Fumbling with her satchel, she pulled her mobile out and turned the flashlight on. A dozen red eyes reflected in the light.

Amari yelped and dropped her phone. Her head told her to run, but her feet wouldn't comply. She stood as if rooted while her heart tried to beat its way out of her chest.

Slowly, she bent down and picked up her phone. Her hand shook so much that someone would probably have mistaken her light for some sort of signal, had anyone been watching. She aimed it into the van again, and her breath hitched into her throat.

Six cages were stacked inside the hold, each containing a white rabbit. They eyed her nervously, their whiskers twitching as they sniffed the air.

"They could be experimenting on them!" Becca's rebuke was like ice down her back.

Not could. Would.

Shooting a glance across her shoulder, and seeing nothing but mist, Amari climbed into the back of the van. She fumbled with the padlock on the first cage. It was sturdy and she knew immediately she wouldn't be able to just wrench it off.

She tried all the cages, but none of them gave in to her frantic tugging and pulling.

Frustrated, Amari closed her eyes, trying to remember what had happened with the lock on the van. She inhaled slowly and, crossing her fingers for luck, exhaled the strange word the voices had whispered to her.

The lock on the first cage clicked open and fell to the floor with a loud clang.

Amari stared at it for a moment.

Then she surged into action, yanking the cage door open. The rabbit needed no further motivation, and Amari took a step back to let it jump out of the cage and scamper out of the van. Amari moved from cage to cage, whispering the word and watching with satisfaction as the little white bodies disappeared into the mist, one after the other.

She was standing in front of the last cage when

she heard voices. Real ones, this time.

"I can give you all six tonight, but if you need something more… exotic… you'll have to wait until tomorrow afternoon," said a man's voice carrying through the mist.

"Six will be enough." Amari recognised Doctor Clarke's voice immediately. "For now."

Fear shot down Amari's spine. She couldn't get caught here. Shooting the last rabbit a regretful look, she darted out of the van and sprinted for the nearest cover. In the mist, she didn't see the shrub until she'd toppled over it. Amari scrambled into place behind it and peered through the leaves just in time to see her supervisor and a lanky man wearing a black trench coat appear out of the mist.

"What the –" the man said when he noticed the van's open doors. He ducked inside and swore loudly.

"Only one left," he growled as he exited the vehicle again, holding up the remaining cage for Doctor Clarke to see. His face was red as he scanned the area and Amari tried to retreat even deeper into the shadows of her hiding place. "Bloody tree-huggers! Must have caught them in the act. They could still be around here…"

"Never mind," Doctor Clarke said, her eyes on the remaining rabbit. "This one will do."

The researcher held her hand out and the man handed her the cage. She handed him a wad of cash in return. They exchanged a few more words, but Amari wasn't listening.

Tristan had been right, and Doctor Clarke was behind it all. Amari knew the university frowned upon animal testing. They might have turned a blind eye to planarians, perhaps even on the mice, but rabbits? Surely what her supervisor was doing was against university policy. Perhaps even illegal.

The sound of the van's engine rumbling to life

startled her back to the moment. She peered through the bushes and saw it drive off, the mist following in its wake until the wall of the lab was clearly visible by the light of the stars.

But there was no sign of Doctor Clarke or her prize.

※※※

Amari pounded on the door of the dorm room next to hers. "Becca!" she whispered fiercely. "Becca, let me in!"

The door across the hall flew open, revealing another student with dishevelled hair and the tired eyes of someone who'd been up all night. "It's two o'clock in the morning!" the girl hissed. "Some of us have finals tomorrow. Keep it down!"

"Sorry," Amari said, wincing.

The girl glared some more at her for good measure before disappearing into her room again.

As quietly as possible, Amari unlocked her own door and tossed her bag onto the floor before falling onto her bed and staring up at the ceiling.

She needed to tell her friend what she'd seen, but Becca clearly wasn't home right now. A twinge of guilt followed that realisation. Her friend could be breaking into Doctor Clarke's storeroom at this very moment. What would she do if she found that rabbit? Would she quietly set it free or, more likely, make a big scene that could get her into trouble?

If it came to a battle of wits, Amari knew Doctor Clarke would have the upper hand – her reputation and her livelihood would be on the line. Her friend stood no chance.

Amari pulled her mobile out and quickly texted Becca.

-- Where are you? I have something to tell you… --

She stared at the screen, willing it to light up with a response, but it stayed frustratingly blank. Then again, if Becca was in the middle of a heist, she wouldn't be stopping to answer texts.

At least Amari had freed most of the rabbits. Her heart ached at the thought of the last one, and the fate that awaited it. No. She shook her head. Perhaps the next version of Doctor Clarke's serum would be a success, and the rabbit would be inconvenienced by nothing more than the small prick of an injection. Amari clung onto that idea as if it was a raft in stormy seas.

She'd go back to the lab tomorrow and see for herself. She owed it that much.

※※※

Becca planted herself in the seat across from Amari at breakfast, slamming her tray loudly on the table. "You're making a mistake, you know," she said, and Amari winced at the hostility in her friend's voice. Becca was spreading butter so forcefully onto her toast that she was poking holes in the crispy bread. "We saw the van last night," she continued. "Coming from Science Area campus, so we were already too late. And we lost it in the mist. What was up with that, anyway?"

Amari shrugged. The weather in this country was so unpredictable, she couldn't tell from one moment to the next what it was going to do. "I know," she said. "I saw it too."

"The mist? There was nothing else to see! Makes it damnably difficult to patrol the area."

"The van."

Amari jumped as Becca's knife clattered onto her plate. "You did? Why didn't you *tell* us?"

"I sent you a text. You didn't answer. I was worried about you."

Becca rolled her eyes. "I was scouting for animal rights abusers. I didn't have *time* for texting. Where was the van when you saw it?"

Lowering her voice, Amari quickly told her friend what had happened the previous night. Becca's face was a portrait of outrage.

"We *need* to set that rabbit free," she demanded in a hushed whisper. "Who knows what might happen to it!" She took a huge bite of toast and, too indignant to worry about good manners, spluttered: "You know they test cosmetics on rabbits, don't you? The poor creature could be subjected to all sorts of powders and lotions and fragrances and who knows what else. It could be covered in a rash *right* now!"

Amari took a sip of her tea, carefully keeping her face neutral. That rabbit was lucky if a rash was the worst of its problems. "I'll go to the labs after breakfast. If I see it, I'll find some way to liberate it," she promised.

"Great," Becca said, downing a glass of orange juice before rising to her feet. "I have a supplementary before lunch. Let me know what happened, okay?"

Amari nodded, wrapping her own slice of bread in a serviette and tucking it into her satchel. A quick visit to the deer in the Grove, and then she'd go finish what she'd started last night.

※※※

Amari's stomach churned and she had to stop for a moment to place her hand on the wall for support as she closed her eyes. Willing her heartbeat to slow down, she forced herself to use her other senses. She could feel the rough texture of the stone beneath her fingers. A bird chirped from a garden hidden out of sight. The smell of roasted coffee drifted from the nearby brewery.

But behind her closed lids, all she could see was the rabbit, grown twice its size and foaming at the mouth, purple veins crisscrossing its hairless body like lightning across a stormy sky, two razor-sharp horns jutting out from its temple, and those angry crimson eyes. It had been attacking the door of its reinforced cage with such vehemence that the shape of its body was outlined in the steel grille.

Amari had done the only thing she could think of under the circumstances – injected it with a lethal dose of morphine that she'd pilfered from Doctor Clarke's stores and watched until the monster's eyes had turned glassy.

It was safe to say that version 74 of the serum hadn't been a success either.

Swallowing back bile, Amari opened her eyes again and stared at the Bodleian library across the road. She still needed to write her paper, and with the deadline looming ever closer, she couldn't afford to get distracted. Her future depended on it, and her family was counting on her.

But she couldn't let this happen to another innocent creature. And the man had said he would have something more 'exotic' by this afternoon. For all Amari knew, Doctor Clarke would be injecting that monstrous serum into one of the Big Five tomorrow. She had to prevent that at all costs.

She needed to get her paper written, and fast, so she could focus on more important things.

⁂

Amari winced as she untucked her leg and

tapped it softly on the cold ground, trying to get some feeling back into it. She'd been too distracted by thoughts of monstrous rhinos running rampant to focus on her studies and had made her way to the labs just as the sun had set to see if Doctor Clarke her received her new test subject yet. The holding room had been empty, so Amari had settled herself into her hiding place behind the bush outside and decided to wait it out.

She glanced at the clock on her mobile. It was close to midnight. Perhaps the van wouldn't be coming tonight, after all.

Goosebumps lifted on her arms and she shivered. She tucked at her scarf before she realised it really wasn't that cold tonight. She looked up to see a mist rolling in from the road. Amari's heart skipped a beat as the black van passed through the gates a moment later and came to a stop a few feet away from her hiding place.

The lanky man she had seen before climbed out of the cab and entered the building.

Amari was on her feet before he had closed the door behind him.

She sprinted towards the van, but paused as the vehicle shook slightly, as if something inside was moving around. Her ears caught a faint noise that sounded almost like neighing. Was there a horse in there?

Amari shrugged. Better than dealing with a rhino.

She whispered the strange word and wrenched the doors open as they unlocked. Amari yelped and jumped backwards as something long and sharp thrust towards her.

Gasping for breath, she stared at the creature, not sure whether she should believe her eyes. It was a horse. Sort of. It was pure white with a silky mane that gleamed in the dim light filtering through the mist. A long ivory horn protruded from the centre of its forehead, shimmering like silver.

Entranced, Amari took a step closer, and then swore and jumped backwards again as the horse thrust its head forward and nearly impaled her with its horn.

She lifted her hands. "Woah, horsey," she whispered in what she hoped was a soothing voice. The horse – unicorn! – stamped its front hoof and shook its head, and Amari noticed the creature's rump was encircled by an iron chain that looped through fixtures welded to the walls of the van. Red welts stood out against the animal's coat where the chain touched it.

"Easy now, easy. I'm not going to hurt you."

The creature stilled and Amari risked taking a step closer, breathing deeply to calm her racing heart. She'd have to win the horse's – unicorn's! – trust first if she wanted to get that chain off.

The animal neighed softly and Amari looked up into its brown eyes. It felt as if time stood still as Amari's mind tried to make sense of the reality of the creature before her. A creature from myth, staring straight back at her. And then it dipped its head forward and Amari felt its velvety coat brush up against her fingers. Goosebumps shot up along her arm. The scent of apples and fresh grass and something she couldn't quite define enveloped her. Amari inhaled deeply and sighed as she felt her shoulders loosen and all her worries fade into a peaceful bliss.

The sound of a door slamming startled her back into the present. Amari's head whipped towards the noise as the unicorn flinched away from her. The lanky man's voice carried through the mist: "Just a sample tonight."

"Yes, yes," Doctor Clarke's voice responded

eagerly. "We can discuss more permanent access once I've analysed it."

Her heart hammering in her ears, Amari stared at the unicorn. There was no time to set it free. She'd be caught and who knew what they'd do to her then? Suddenly, failing philosophy didn't seem like the worst thing that could happen to her anymore. Casting the unicorn a regretful look, Amari shoved the van's doors closed and sprinted towards her hiding place. She'd be no use to the animal if she got caught tonight.

She dived behind the bush just in time. She peered through the brush to see the lanky man and Doctor Clarke emerge from the swirling mist. The man opened the van doors and the researcher gasped.

"Magnificent," she breathed, stepping coolly to the side as the creature lunged towards her with its horn and then fell back again as the chain stopped its impetus. "I must admit, Mister Dawson, I hadn't quite believed you before now. And it has healing properties, you say?"

"That is the common consensus," the man replied, nodding. He stretched a warning hand out as the unicorn struggled against her bonds. "Come now, Una darling, you know this hurts me more than it hurts you." He stepped closer and said something under his breath that Amari couldn't make out and she watched in amazement as the unicorn suddenly stood still, motionless as a statue, only her eyes rolling wildly in their sockets.

The lanky man nodded towards Doctor Clarke and the woman pulled a syringe from her pocket. "You sure this is safe?" She eyed the immobile creature dubiously.

"Quite safe."

The researcher carefully moved closer, and when the unicorn still didn't move, she placed the syringe against the animal's neck and quickly drew a blood sample. With practiced ease, Doctor Clarke sealed the glass tube and held it up to the light. The blood inside glinted a deep shade of purple.

"I'll analyse this in the morning, and if your claims prove to be true…" Doctor Clarke's mouth twisted into a shrewd pout. "Well, then we can discuss a more permanent arrangement."

"Of course," the man – Dawson – said, closing the van doors again. "I'll expect to hear from you soon."

They said their farewells, and Dawson climbed into the van and drove off. Amari watched Doctor Clarke stare after it as the mist faded, an unreadable expression on her face and her hand clamped around the vial of blood. Then she turned on her heels and disappeared into the lab building.

Amari sat back, breathing hard. A unicorn! When she closed her eyes, she could still smell its magical scent and feel the softness of its coat against her skin. She could still remember the way it had looked at her, as if seeing straight into her soul.

What would Doctor Clarke find in its blood? Could it be the key to unlocking the cure she had been so desperately searching for? And if so, what would happen to the unicorn?

Whatever happened next, Amari needed to make sure that the unicorn did not share that rabbit's fate. Her hands shook as she pushed herself to her feet. She would not let *anything* happen to that unicorn. Not now, not ever. No matter what.

⁂

"Miss Kerubo?"

Amari gazed into the distance, her surroundings blurring as her mind's eye superimposed memories from the previous night upon her vision. Her focus pinpointed upon a single image of a shimmering white horse with a sparkling silver horn jutting from its forehead, its soft brown eyes a sea of tranquillity that washed over her, leaving her with a profound sense of serenity.

"Miss Kerubo?"

If she concentrated hard enough, she could see herself walking beside the unicorn, perhaps in a moonlit grove with stars twinkling above and flowers blooming in their footsteps, the air thick with the sweet perfume of lilies. Amari would tangle her fingers in the unicorn's silky mane and they would be at peace, knowing they were both safe. A smile played across her lips.

"Amari!"

Amari started as reality forced itself upon her, and she blinked the classroom back into focus. Across from her, Professor Wallace glared at her over her half-moon glasses, and behind the podium beside her, Jennifer Brody stared at her as if she were some sort of simpleton. Amari coughed, embarrassed. She couldn't believe she'd zoned out in the middle of the debate!

"Would you care to respond to Miss Brody's remark, Miss Kerubo?" Professor Wallace enquired acerbically, tapping her red pen irritably against the notepad spread out on the desk before her.

Amari swallowed. "I'm sorry, but could you repeat it, please?" She wanted to kick herself. Her marks for politics this semester weren't good enough to afford brushing this debate off. She could use every bit of extra credit on offer.

Jennifer repeated her statement, and Amari

sighed with relief. She responded with something that seemed to satisfy Professor Wallace, who grunted as she returned her attention to the other student.

Amari let herself relax again. Jennifer's words were like white noise as her thoughts drifted to the vial of blood Doctor Clarke had claimed. Should she try to steal it from the labs? No, Amari discarded that thought immediately. Better to let the woman do her analysis and see what the outcome is. Perhaps the results would be negative and the unicorn would be safe from any further experimentation.

"Your thoughts, Miss Kerubo?"

Amari clamped her jaw as she realised she'd once again not paid attention. Frantically, she wracked her brain for any hints. Had Jennifer said something about voting rights for non-resident nationals, or improving rights for resident non-nationals? She snorted. The girl lived three doors down from her and had never given her so much as a good morning. She went with the first option.

"Very good," Professor Wallace said in a tone of voice that indicated quite the opposite.

Amari fidgeted behind her podium while the woman scribbled frantically on her notepad. Nervously clenching and unclenching her fists, she glanced sideways to see Jennifer smirking self-confidently. Finally, after what felt like a lifetime, Professor Wallace looked up again and said: "Miss Brody, excellent argumentative skills and a clear knowledge of the current political climate. Miss Kerubo, adequate counterarguments, but lacking both focus and conviction. The extra credit will go to Miss Brody."

Amari's shoulders slumped as Jennifer shot her a haughty look. Glumly, she packed up her satchel and followed the other girl towards the door, but just as she was about to leave the room, Professor Wallace cleared her throat loudly.

"Miss Kerubo, a word."

Amari returned to the teacher's desk. The woman managed to look down upon Amari over her spectacles, even though she was seated. Her lined face was drawn into a disapproving frown.

"I don't say this often to my students, Miss Kerubo, but I think you should reconsider your field of study. Politics is clearly not where your interest lies." Professor Wallace tapped her red pen irritably against the notepad. "You're wasting both my time and yours."

"I'm sorry," Amari stammered, her voice barely audible. Shame heated her face as she tried to look everywhere but into those judgemental eyes.

The woman grunted. "Life is too short for half-measures, Miss Kerubo. Find your focus, whatever it may be, and pursue if with single-minded intent. Anything else is just a waste of time. You may go."

Swallowing back the sudden lump in her throat, Amari hitched her satchel over her shoulder again and fled the room.

※※※

The atmosphere was subdued in The Tenth Muse as Amari nursed a cup of chamomile tea. It wasn't the rooibos she preferred, but it was the closest substitute she could get on such short notice in this foreign country. Her mood was sombre as she reflected on Professor Wallace's words.

The woman was right, of course, but it was uncomfortable to hear the truth she had tried to avoid for so long spoken so plainly. Amari had spent the past three years of her life pursuing a dream her family had cherished on her behalf. Could she really let them down now, when she was so close to the end goal?

Could she follow their dream instead of hers?

She shook her head. That line of thought would get her nowhere until she first figured out what she wanted to do with her life. Professor Wallace had been right again: she lacked focus. She was like a sunbird flitting from flower to flower, always tasting but never stopping for a more satisfying draught.

Taking another sip of tea, Amari glared at the dog-eared research paper Professor Bottenfeldt had given her. Reading it had been like watching a train slowly derailing, unable to prevent the author from reaching his inevitable conclusion. But she had to admit – Davids might not know myth from truth, but at least he was passionate about his subject matter.

Amari pushed the paper and the disappointing cup of tea to the side as her mobile pinged. It was a text from Doctor Clarke.

-- Success at last! Come to the lab if you can. I need a second pair of eyes. --

She stared at the screen for a moment, not sure if she should be relieved or terrified. She opted for alarmed, packed up her things as quickly as she could and set off towards the labs at a half-trot.

Doctor Clarke was grinning like the Cheshire Cat when Amari walked through the door. The woman beckoned her over impatiently and moved out of the way so Amari could look into the microscope she had set up.

Amari refocussed the lens. "Looks like damaged tissue cells," she said.

"Very good," Doctor Clarke replied. "Now look at this."

The end of a pipette appeared in Amari's field of vision, depositing a reddish-purple liquid into the dish. Amari gasped. As soon as the fluid came into contact with a damaged cell, the cell took on a vibrant pink colour and started to rapidly regenerate until it was completely healed. When that cell collided with another one, it changed colour and repaired itself too, until the entire dish was practically squirming with robust, thriving cells.

"That's… that's amazing," Amari breathed, pulling away from the microscope.

"Isn't it just!" Doctor Clarke threw her hands excitedly into the air. "It's the miracle I've been waiting for!"

"What did you change in the formula?"

The researcher sobered up quickly. She pulled the dish out from underneath the microscope and quickly sealed it up. "The formula remains unchanged," she said, avoiding eye contact. "This is a… reactive agent I recently acquired. Unfortunately, it's incredibly scarce. I'll need to dilute it somehow and incorporate it into the serum for mass production."

Amari licked her lips, her mouth suddenly dry. Unicorn blood. She'd been looking at the effect of pure unicorn blood on injured cells. With such astonishing results, Doctor Clarke would want a lifetime supply of it.

"Can't you reverse engineer the agent? Maybe synthetically recreate it?"

Doctor Clarke shook her head, and Amari immediately realised why: the unicorn was a creature of myth. If she hadn't seen it with her own eyes, caressed its glossy coat with her fingertips, Amari would be screaming to all who'd listen that such a thing didn't exist, no matter what the old stories said, and no matter what someone like that scholar, James Davids, might believe.

But it did exist.

And it must defy all the laws of science. Its blood was probably infused with magical properties the likes of which you'd never find on the periodic table. If Doctor Clarke wanted her healing serum, she was going to need to get it directly from the source.

"What's next?" Amari asked as she watched her supervisor carefully label the petri dish before putting it into a small cooler box.

"Live subject testing," Doctor Clarke replied distractedly. "I'm expecting another batch of rabbits tomorrow. Meanwhile, I'll need to write up my findings. Perhaps now that I have positive results, I can get my research grant renewed." She pulled her notebook closer and started jotting a few words down. "I'll need a full-time assistant, too. You're finishing your degree this year, aren't you? I could recommend you for the position. That should be sufficient motivation to have your student visa extended." The woman looked enquiringly at Amari.

Amari stared back at her, at a loss for words. This could be the answer to all her problems. She'd be able to change her degree and stay at Oxford for at least another year. There would be no need to go back to her family with empty hands.

All she'd had to do was be willing to experiment with unicorn blood.

"I'll... get back to you on that," she said, wincing at the surprised look on her supervisor's face.

"You don't want to be a part of this? Amari, did you *see* those cells? They were healing themselves!"

"Of course," she blurted. "It's just... I'll need

to change my major. And… I don't know what Professor Harris would say –"

Doctor Clarke waved Amari's concerns away. "Oh, pish posh! Don't worry about that. I'll handle all the paperwork. I want you by my side, Amari. You're my best student, no matter what the marks say. You're a natural."

Amari cleared her throat uncomfortably. If only the woman knew what she was planning. She'd chase her out of the lab without a second thought.

Her doubts must have been visible on her face, because Doctor Clarke sighed theatrically and said: "Okay, fine, take some time to think about it. But don't take too long. Now that I know it's possible, I'll want to start producing something that I can show to the committee." Her cheeks flushed pink and it was all Amari could do not to grab her bag and run out of the lab.

Instead, she mumbled something about still needing to write her paper and excused herself. The researcher barely noticed, her thoughts undoubtedly already far into the future as she scribbled frantically in her notebook.

Outside, Amari took a deep breath of fresh air to calm her racing nerves. If she wanted to protect the unicorn, she'd need to locate the lanky man – Dawson – and figure out where he kept the animal. Once she'd found it, she'd figure out what to do next.

But first, she needed to find that unmarked van. And she knew someone who might just be able to help.

※※※

"There's nothing as incongruous as an African guy sitting in the nave of Christ Church Cathedral playing shooter games on his laptop."

Phumlani pulled one earphone out as he looked up from his game. "That's exactly why I do it," he said, flashing Amari a dazzling smile. "Plus, this is the fastest Wi-Fi spot on campus." He shrugged. "What's a guy to do?"

His brows wrinkled as she sat down on the hard pew beside him, and he closed his laptop and pulled the other earpiece out, too. "*Eish*, something tells me you haven't come to reminisce about home today."

Amari shook her head. "I have a favour to ask. But it could get you in trouble." A spark of interest flared in his eyes. "Just say no if you're not comfortable doing it. I'll understand completely."

"I haven't said no yet, have I?"

Amari looked around the cathedral, careful of who might overhear their conversation. There were only a few tourists about this close to lunchtime, and they were all intent on their e-guides, dutifully wandering from one checkpoint to the next as a voice in their ears tried its best to make history, religion, and architecture palatable to the masses.

She lowered her voice anyway. "There was an unmarked van outside the biology labs last night, around midnight. I was wondering if you could tell me who it belongs to. Or where it went."

Phumlani jumped to his feet, nearly sending his laptop flying. "Finally!" he exclaimed. "This is exactly why I went into IT!"

Amari tried to sink into the hard wooden bench as all eyes turned towards them. Even the gargoyles, perched high underneath the soaring Gothic arches, seemed to judge them right now.

Abashed, Phumlani sat back down again. He leaned in close to her, his stage whisper loud enough to carry to the other side of the cathedral.

"Are you a recruiter? Is this the test that'll get me into MI6?" He was practically bouncing on his seat with pent-up excitement. "I know 007 is taken already, but can I be 008? Or will I be working with Q instead?"

Amari laughed. "You know that's just fiction, right?"

"Right," he agreed, winking.

Amari shook her head, chuckling. "I'm sorry to disappoint, but this is a private request. I don't know anything about MI6."

"No, of course not," Phumlani laughed easily. "But we can pretend, right?"

"Sure," Amari shrugged as he flipped his laptop open again and started typing furiously. She peered at the screen. Text boxes popped up and closed again faster than she could make sense of them. "What are you doing?"

"Hacking into the surveillance cameras." His fingers flew across the keyboard as he scrolled through a series of folders and files that made no sense to Amari's uninitiated eyes.

"I don't want you to get into trouble," she said again. "Are you sure no one will be able to trace what you're doing?"

"The only person good enough to trace what I'm doing here is me," Phumlani replied confidently. "Midnight last night, right?" he asked, his brows knitting together. "There's only static."

"That's… not very helpful," Amari replied. "Is there something wrong with that camera?"

"No, look." Phumlani sped the video up until the image suddenly cleared. There was nothing to see but the side of the building. The date stamp in the corner showed only a few minutes after midnight. Phumlani rewound the feed and Amari watched the static with bated breath until the feed cleared again, still showing nothing suspicious. She glanced at the time in the corner. A quarter to midnight.

"That's when the van showed up," she said, her eyes widening. "The static coincides with the van!"

Phumlani lifted an eyebrow at her. "You think it has some kind of signal jammer or something?"

"Or something," Amari breathed, thinking of the unicorn. "Can you check the night before?"

Phumlani's fingers flew across the keyboard. Another grainy black and white video opened on the screen.

Amari's pulse quickened as a van drove into view and stopped with its rear end just within shot of the camera. A few seconds later, a tall man wearing a trench coat walked into the frame, his features obscured by mist suddenly swirling around the vehicle. The man disappeared into the building. Phumlani sped the feed up until someone else also walked into view.

"Is that you?" he asked, peering at the figure whose face, thankfully, was turned away from the camera. "Wait, are you breaking into that van?"

"You can speed it up again," Amari said, avoiding his eyes. "I want to know what happens after it drives off again."

Pursing his lips, Phumlani complied and the security footage sped forward until Amari saw herself stepping out of the van. Her face was pixelated, but anyone who knew her would have recognised her. Phumlani said nothing, but she noticed a tightness in his posture as he leaned ever so slightly away from her.

"There," she said as two other figures stepped into view. Mist swirled in front of the camera, obscuring their faces. Amari grunted, annoyed. Then the black shadow of the van passed in front of the camera again, before the mist dissolved, leaving the view towards the lab unobscured.

Phumlani closed the screen and turned towards her. "I know I said I'd help, but if you're doing something illegal –"

"I'm not," Amari quickly interrupted. "It's an animal smuggling ring. I was setting rabbits free."

"That's all?" he asked, folding his arms across his chest. "Because that seems like a stupid thing to risk your visa for, and I know you're not stupid."

Amari hesitated. She'd asked him to risk his visa for her. She owed him the truth. A troubled sigh escaped her lips. "My research supervisor is experimenting on animals. She's working on a formula – a serum that's supposed to enhance the regenerative attributes of self-healing species to see if she can find some kind of super cure for replacing or regenerating damaged tissue or organs. Before today, all she's managed is to turn her test subjects into monsters." She shuddered, the rabbit's red eyes haunting her again. "And when I say monsters, I mean that quite literally."

Phumlani's eyes widened, and a low whistle escaped his lips. "Amari, if I didn't know you better, I'd say you were high on *umqombothi*. Are you serious?"

Amari nodded. "I can't let her do that to another innocent animal," she continued. "No matter how well-intentioned her objectives are. The animals deserve to be protected. And I need you to help me find her supplier and put an end to it." She decided not to mention the unicorn. She needed his help, not his scepticism.

Phumlani swore beneath his breath and then looked guiltily around the cathedral to see if someone had noticed. He turned back to the laptop. "Alright, let's see what we can find. This mist isn't helping. Is this even natural?"

Amari relaxed back into the pew again as Phumlani attacked his keyboard once more. Her eyes lifted towards the stained-glass windows and the kaleidoscope of colours filtering through them, casting a mystical ambience around the two of them. She felt her shoulders relax as dappled rainbow colours danced about her.

"Yes!" Phumlani pumped a fist into the air, shattering Amari's reverie. "Eat your heart out, MI6."

Amari turned her attention back to the screen. A series of windows were open, all showing grainy security feeds. Amari watched as the mist moved from one feed to the next. "You followed the mist."

"You make it sound so simple," Phumlani said, wincing. "It's a complicated algorithm, even for me. I had to –"

"Yes, and it's amazing and you're a genius and the greatest geek I know," Amari said impatiently. "I don't need to know how you did it. Where did it go?"

"Follow the white rabbit," Phumlani replied. They watched as the mist moved across screens, finally dissipating to reveal the van parked in a side street next to a pet shop. Tacky gold lettering painted on the window said *Dawson & Son's Exotic Pet Emporium.*

Amari's jaw ached from clenching it as she stared at the sign. Dawson.

"What're you going to do now?" Phumlani asked.

She took a deep breath. "I guess it's time to become an activist."

⁂

Amari was reconsidering her life choices as she stood in the shadows of an alley that smelled strongly of old beer and urine, watching the van's owner close and lock up the shop. She should have been inside a library writing a paper about ethics. Instead, she was dressed in dark hues and about to trespass onto, and quite possibly burglarise, a pet shop.

Her parents would be so proud.

"That's the van, alright," Tristan said in a low voice. "Well done, Amari."

Becca flashed her a quick smile. "Now remember," she said as they watched the man saunter off, probably heading towards the nearest pub. "No touching anything without these on." She pulled three sets of black leather gloves from her backpack and handed a pair each to Amari and Tristan. "What we're doing tonight is definitely *not* legal, so I'd rather not leave fingerprints everywhere."

A bitter taste filled Amari's mouth. "And what about that?" She pointed at the security camera mounted to the wall opposite the pet shop and aimed directly at its front door, which was illuminated by a spotlight hanging from the roof two storeys higher. There was no way they could avoid being seen.

"That's what these are for," Tristan said as he pulled a balaclava across his face. He held another one out to her.

Amari took it reluctantly. "Isn't this a bit... obvious?" Her friends stared at her. "I mean, if we get caught, we could still somehow talk our way out of it, but not while wearing these. These make it pretty clear that we're up to no good."

"We won't get caught," Becca said, slipping her balaclava across her head. "Tristan's done this many times before."

"And was caught! Twice, if I remember correctly."

"We won't get caught." Tristan sounded calm and confident, but Amari noticed how he bounced on the balls of his feet. He was as nervous as she was.

She glared at the balaclava. It was going to completely ruin her hair. "How are we going to get in, anyway?"

"With this." Becca pulled a crowbar from her backpack.

"No." Amari shook her head. "No way."

"Do you have any better ideas?" Tristan snapped.

Amari bit her lower lip, contemplating an idea. "As a matter of fact, I do." She pressed the balaclava into Becca's hands and quickly crossed the street before her friends, and her better judgement, could object.

Keeping her face averted from the camera, she walked up to the pet shop door and bent over the handle, as if she was trying to unlock it with a key. Instead, she whispered the word that had unlocked the rabbit cages. A thrill of excitement shot down her spine as the lock clicked and the handle gave way beneath her fingers. She pushed the door open and slipped into the shop.

It took a moment for her eyes to adjust to the dim light. It was a small shop, cluttered with cages lined up against three of the four walls, and a row of fish tanks in the middle, making it even more cramped. She could see a counter with a till at the back of the room, with a door in the wall behind it. The stench of rat pee and pet food soured the air.

"I didn't know you were so good at lock picking," Tristan said behind her. "You should show me how you did that some time."

Amari shrugged. "What's the plan?"

"We free stuff." Becca pushed a pair of pliers into Amari's hands and walked towards the nearest cage. A slight clang followed as she snipped a wire.

"Aww, look, there's a chinchilla in this one."

Amari turned towards Tristan. "What happens to the animals if we set them free? They can't just run loose in the streets. Isn't there someone from your organisation that can come pick them up?"

He shook his head, worrying at the lock of a cage housing a dispirited-looking teacup pig. "We'd need due cause to remove the animals. Unless you want to go through the place's financial records and look for something to show illegal activity, this is our best option."

Amari frowned. Perhaps she hadn't thought this through enough. She'd only cared about finding the unicorn and getting the other animals away from here. Away to where hadn't occurred to her until just now.

Guiltily leaving her friends to liberate the animals, she shoved the pliers into the back pocket of her jeans and headed for the counter at the back. The shelves were stacked with everything from anti-fungal cream to cure-all ointments promising to make feathers fluffier and scales shinier. She rifled through the drawers, looking for anything suspicious. Her gaze landed on a small vial containing a thick red liquid with a purple sheen to it that looked exactly like the sample Doctor Clarke had taken from the unicorn.

Amari's heart thumped loudly in her ears as she pocketed the vial. Proof they were in the right place. She surveyed the shop again, where Becca and Tristan were still enthusiastically breaking cages open. Obviously, no unicorn here.

She turned towards the door in the back. It had a small window inset through which Amari could see steps leading down to a basement. Maybe that was where Dawson kept the 'exotic' animals. She pictured a room filled with crates containing lions and pangolins, then shook her head. If exotic meant unicorn, who knew what was in there?

Amari tried the handle. The moment her hand touched the cool steel, a flashing red light caught her eye. She looked up to see a security camera in the ceiling pointing at her.

She swore under her breath. "We need to get out of here. Now!"

The sound of something metallic falling into place startled her. Becca shrieked and Amari sprinted towards the front of the shop to see her friends gaping at each other. A steel security gate had slid across the door and the shop window, locking them in as if they were in a cage themselves. Amari pulled her pair of pliers out again and swore under her breath. They would be no match for those thick bars.

Tristan pushed past Becca, who stood frozen as if in shock, her eyes wide behind her balaclava. He wrenched at the barricade, but it didn't budge. Frantically, he rushed around the room, looking in vain for another exit.

The sound of police sirens jolted Amari into action. She couldn't be caught here tonight! She lunged at the security gate, hissing the word that had opened the door earlier. A feint click told her something had happened. She tried to lift the steel gate, but it was too heavy.

"Tristan," she called. "Help me lift this!"

The young activist was beside her in an instant, wedging his shoulder underneath a horizontal bar. His face contorted as he tried to heave the gate upwards. It lifted an inch before Tristan let it drop again, his face red.

The screech of sirens became deafening and blue lights flickering on top of a car coming to a stop outside the shop declared their time was up. A ball of molten lead churned in Amari's stomach. She could practically see someone stamp the word

'Denied' in bold red letters on her passport.

Turning on her heels, she fled towards the back of the shop. She dropped to her knees and tried to squeeze into a space between the counter and an enormous bag of dog food pellets, hoping she'd be overlooked in the confusion, when her hand touched something cold and scaly. Amari recoiled. In the flashing red light of the security camera, she could see a snake slithering towards her, its sinuous coils undulating across the linoleum.

With a yelp, she jumped to her feet and sprinted away from the snake as fast as she could, and straight into the arms of a policeman.

"Now, now, Miss," he said, holding onto her with one hand while he flicked the light switch on. His eyes widened as he saw the freed animals that hadn't escaped yet dashing around the room. "A right mess you've caused, haven't you?"

Amari's gaze darted towards the door. Becca, her hair dishevelled and her balaclava in one hand, leaned on the arm of another policeman. Her face was pale, and she looked about ready to faint.

"I know there's three of you," the officer called, ushering Amari towards her friend. "Don't make me get my pepper spray out."

Reluctantly, Tristan stepped out from behind the wall of fish tanks. He pulled the balaclava from his head, and the policeman snickered.

"Mister Ford! Fancy meeting you here." The officer stepped in closer and slapped a pair of handcuffs around Tristan's wrists. "It's been a month or two since you last graced our cells with your presence."

Tristan's lips curled into a sneer, but he kept quiet.

"Go on, then," the chatty policeman said as his silent friend led the three of them towards their car. In the glare of the flashing lights, Amari could see a crowd gathered around the vehicle, gaping at the spectacle. She cringed as she recognised Professor Bottenfeldt in the throng.

"Watch your head."

Amari was last to climb into the back of the car, wincing as the door slammed shut in her face. The silent cop slid behind the wheel, while his friend turned around to jeer at them. "I hope you don't have any exams in the morning. It's going to be a long night."

Amari sighed. She did have an exam in the morning.

But as the car pulled away from the shop, she couldn't help but stare at the tacky lettering on the window. Why would a shoddy pet shop have a silent alarm in the back, but not on the front door? An alarm that brought the cops running if you only touched a doorhandle.

If she'd had any doubts before, she was even more sure now that the door led to the unicorn. Amari clenched her fists. If she was going to lose her visa after tonight, it had better be worth it. She was going to find that unicorn if it was the last thing she did.

⁂

The clanging of a key turning in a rusty lock awakened Amari the next morning. She glanced at the clock on the wall outside her cell. It was ten in the morning, and she'd already missed her exam.

"Out you go, girly," the female officer said, holding the door open for her. "You're lucky. The owner decided not to press any charges. You're free to go."

She rolled off the steel bench she had spent an uncomfortable night on. While Becca's parents had come to bail her out not long after they'd arrived at the precinct, and a surly-looking friend did the same for Tristan an hour or two later, Amari had had no one to come to her aid. She'd spent the night alternately berating herself for being so stupid and feeling sorry for herself.

She stretched the cramps out of her shoulders before following the officer to the front, where they had her sign a release form before returning her phone and purse – they kept the pliers – and promptly shooing her out of the station with a warning to not do anything reckless again.

Standing underneath the cloudy sky, Amari wondered what to do next. She'd had a lucky escape, and in the clear light of day, she was suddenly unsure whether it was it worth risking her future for the unicorn's sake. Come to think of it, had she really seen a *unicorn*? Surely not. Maybe her overstressed mind had been playing tricks on her. Maybe she was subconsciously trying to self-sabotage. Maybe she was just as crazy as that academic, Davids, was. Her mood was sombre by the time she reached her room at Magdalen.

She'd just had time to brush the taste of jail cell out of her mouth when her mobile phone pinged. Her breath hitched in her throat as she read the text message.

-- *Come see me. NOW please.* --

She squirted some fragrance on her wrists and practically ran out of her room and across campus where she paused, breathless, to straighten her hair before she knocked on the office door of her academic advisor.

"Come," a stern voice called from behind the closed door. Amari entered to see Professor Harris glaring at her from across his desk.

"Miss Kerubo," he said, his lips turning down

in disapproval. "Please, sit down."

She took a seat across from him and waited in uncomfortable silence as he scribbled on a piece of paper. Finally, Professor Harris pushed the document aside and fixed an icy stare on her.

"Do you know what I've just been writing, Miss Kerubo?"

Amari shook her head, but her fingers tugged nervously at the scarf around her neck.

Professor Harris tapped a finger irritably on the piece of paper. "This, Miss Kerubo, is a letter in which I have previously recommended your student visa to be extended for another year for postgraduate studies, but which I now unfortunately have had to modify, in the absence of a final paper and considering your abysmal philosophy marks this semester. Not to mention the call I received from the police department last night. And if I'm not mistaken, you also missed an exam this morning."

Amari's mouth went dry. "You're recommending that my visa be revoked?"

The exam she'd missed was for an elective that wouldn't count towards her final mark. It didn't matter. But she'd been harbouring ideas of changing her focus towards a major in classical studies next year, with the vague idea of going into academics afterwards. If her student visa was revoked, she'd have no choice but to return to South Africa where, with no degree behind her name, she'd be looking at a soulless office job at best, and unemployment more likely. She'd never be approved for another bursary if she dropped out of a prestigious university such as this with nothing to show for it.

Suddenly, Doctor Clarke's offer looked much more appealing. But would she still want Amari as her assistant after what had happened last night?

"I am," Professor Harris said. "Unless you somehow manage to pull a rabbit out of a hat." He fixed her with a piercing glare. "Reputations must be upheld, Miss Kerubo. We cannot allow anyone to continue associating with this university without merit. Do you understand?"

Fighting back a sense of impending doom, Amari muttered: "I still have time. The paper is only due by midnight."

Professor Harris grunted. "You'll need nothing short of a miracle, Miss Kerubo. If I were you, I'd be praying for some divine intervention right about now."

Amari's shoulders slumped. Her entire future rested on that final paper. The one she still hadn't even started. She had no choice but to forget about Doctor Clarke's experiments and concentrate on getting that paper written. Nothing else mattered right now.

Professor Harris studied her for a few moments, and then he huffed. "Very well. I will leave the paperwork for later. Don't give me a reason to sign that document and send you packing."

"Yes, sir," Amari said, rising to her feet.

She closed the office door behind her, breathing a sigh of relief at how close she'd come to shaming her family. A tightness formed in her chest as she walked through the administrative wing. She still did not know what to write about, and she was quickly running out of time. Normally, the idea of spending the evening in the library would have been appealing, but the very thought of needing to reread those tedious eighteenth-century philosophers again slowed her steps down until she wasn't so much walking as trudging in the general direction of the library.

She needed to get some fresh air first. A quick

visit to the deer at the Grove would revive her spirits before she resigned herself to her fate.

She hastened her steps towards the park, but slowed down as she saw someone else already standing at the fence, looking out over the herd. Amari's footsteps faltered. It was Doctor Clarke.

The woman turned and saw Amari. She beckoned her over.

Reluctantly, Amari walked closer, shoving her hands into the pockets of her jacket. She frowned as she felt something round and cool. The vial of purple liquid! The police had missed it when they'd searched her last night and she'd forgotten about it in all the excitement.

She hadn't imagined anything. She really had seen a unicorn. And Doctor Clarke was experimenting with its blood.

Amari swallowed nervously as she joined her mentor. How had she never noticed the glint of cruelty in the woman's eyes before? The researcher tapped a manicured fingernail against her cheek as she contemplated the animals grazing on the new spring grass.

"It's sick, that one."

Amari looked towards the deer Doctor Clarke was pointing at. Her breath hitched in her throat as she recognised the little fawn with the diamond-shaped patch between its ears. "How can you tell?" she stammered.

"Look at the way it's walking. It's swaying like a drunken sailor. See the drooping ears?"

Amari felt her teeth grind together as she clenched her jaw. The woman was right; the fawn did look off balance. She bit her lower lip, trying to stay calm. "What will you do?"

Doctor Clarke glanced at her. "Oh, nothing," she said. Then she winked, before putting her hands in her pockets and sauntering off.

A bitter taste filled Amari's mouth. There was nothing she could do. If Doctor Clarke was going to experiment on the fawn, the best Amari could hope for is that the unicorn's blood failed to cure it. She felt sorry for the little animal, but better it died naturally than prove the researcher right and stoke her lust for the mythical creature's blood.

Amari clenched her fists. She needed to put a stop to this. She needed to find the unicorn.

But she also needed to write her paper. And she *would* get the damn thing written before the deadline tonight.

But she couldn't do it all alone. She pulled out her mobile phone.

-- *I need another favour. Are you up to the challenge?* --

Phumlani's response was almost immediate.

-- *Is the Pope Catholic?* --

Amari smiled. She quickly typed out her request before taking a deep breath and setting off towards the library.

⁂

She was just walking past the Radcliffe Camera when her phone started ringing. It was Becca.

"Oh, thank goodness, Amari!" her friend's voice was filled with relief. "I was afraid you'd still be locked up in that dreadful cell. When did you get out?"

"This morning," Amari replied, surprised at the hint of bitterness in her voice. She couldn't help but feel resentful at the ease with which her friend had escaped their predicament. She hadn't slept in a holding cell all night. Nobody had threatened *Becca* with deportation.

On the other side of the line, Becca gasped theatrically. "How terrible! It's an *outrage*, really. They had no right! I mean, sure, we were caught trespassing, but we hadn't stolen anything. Alright, maybe a few animals escaped, but really, they shouldn't be keeping them in cages like that, anyway. Really, we should demand compensation for all the mental anguish *we* suffered last night! Not to mention the damage to our reputations! Did you see how many people were watching when the police manhandled us into their car? In fact, I think I should march down to the station right now and –"

"Yeah, listen Becca," Amari interrupted her friend. "I desperately need to get my paper written. Meet up with you and Tristan tomorrow night for drinks?"

Becca snorted audibly. "Oh, Tristan and I are so over! Can you believe he had the gall to call me up and ask for money to pay his friend back? I can't believe I let him dazzle me into almost having a criminal record. I'm about to graduate with a *law* degree! No, I can do better than some secondary school dropout pretending to be a bad boy saving the planet. All he really does is get others into trouble! I mean –"

"Good for you," Amari said quickly. "Tell me all about it tomorrow, alright?"

Becca huffed. "Alright, go write your paper. See you on the flip side."

She ended the call, and Amari stared at the dead phone for a moment. Had her friend always been such a flake? She'd probably never cared about the animals at all. They were just another distraction for Becca to briefly champion and then forget about.

Amari was still looking at the mobile when its

screen lit up again with a text message.

-- *I'm in.* --

Her eyes widened in surprise. She looked up at the library door across the road and then at the clock displayed on her phone. There was still time.

Pocketing her mobile, she turned her back on the library and hurried down the street towards Christ Church Cathedral.

※※※

"What did you find?" Amari whispered as she slid onto the pew next to Phumlani. It was lunchtime and the cathedral was exceptionally full today. Tourists wandered the aisles while students made temporarily pious by exam time cluttered the nave.

The hacker turned his laptop so she could peer at the grainy black and white feed on the screen. It showed a bare windowless room –the pet shop's basement. Completely empty.

Amari frowned. "You sure this is the right feed?"

Phumlani snorted. "Of course I'm sure. There are only three cameras hooked up to this network." He counted them on his fingers: "The one outside the shop, the one pointing at the door you mentioned, and the one inside this room."

"But why would they have a camera inside an empty room? And one watching the door leading to it. It doesn't make sense."

"Beats me, but I've scrolled through a week's worth of feed and there was nothing to see. Except…" he paused theatrically.

Amari tapped her foot impatiently on the stone floor. "Go on."

"Two nights ago, not long after midnight."

Her breath hitched in her throat. "That was the same night… What did you see?"

"Nothing," Phumlani said, opening a minimised video feed so Amari could see. "Just static. Again." He looked at her significantly.

"You think whatever was causing the disturbance when the van passed the other security cameras also caused it here? It was in this room?" Amari tapped a finger against her cheek. All the evidence suggested that the unicorn had been in that basement shortly after she'd seen the van leave the labs. "But where is it now?" she asked aloud.

The hacker shrugged. "No idea." He forwarded the feed again until the image cleared to show the empty basement again. "I haven't seen anyone come or go into this room. It's a mystery."

Amari chewed on her bottom lip. If the unicorn had been in that basement, she would have broken into that pet shop again tonight to rescue it somehow, but the creature must be long gone by now. It was out of her reach.

"Thanks, anyway," she said, rising to her feet. "I owe you one."

"No worries," Phumlani replied. "008, remember." He winked at her.

Amari laughed as she left the cathedral and reluctantly traipsed back towards the library.

※※※

Silence hung oppressively over the stacks of the Bodleian library. Students with red-rimmed eyes filled every seat, some frantically typing on their laptops, while others tried their best to get as much reading done before exhaustion claimed them. Three rows down from Amari, a guy sprawled across a desk, snoring softly.

In a quiet nook tucked away at the back, she yawned as she crumpled yet another piece of paper into a ball and pushed it towards the pile of discarded attempts amassed at one corner of her desk. She slumped back into her chair, frustrated. Why could she not think of anything coherent to write? She closed her eyes and rubbed at the throbbing ache at her temples. It was a lost cause. She was going to get deported, and there was nothing she could do about it.

"Still wrestling with the muse, Miss Kerubo?"

Amari wished she could fold into herself and disappear behind the stack of books she had accumulated on her desk. The last time Professor Bottenfeldt had seen her, she'd been in the back of a police car.

"She's proven to be quite elusive so far," Amari sighed as she opened her eyes to see the professor standing before her, his arms folded across his chest.

"Perhaps you've been searching for her in the wrong places?"

Amari's gaze snapped to his, wondering if he was alluding to her botched burglary. His watery blue eyes gave no clue to his thoughts.

"I've been… distracted," she admitted.

"Not an uncommon occurrence," he chuckled. "You've been searching for your calling for a long time now, Amari. The question is, is this distraction a temporary diversion, or is it worth pursuing?"

Amari's thoughts bounced off the unicorn before flitting back to the rabbit, and the mouse before that. She shuddered. "It's worth pursuing." Professor Bottenfeldt nodded, and she couldn't help but sense that he was somehow pleased by her answer. "But I'll need a miracle to get this paper done by midnight, and if I don't, Professor Harris has threatened to revoke my student visa."

"Well, we can't have that now," the professor said, tugging thoughtfully on the hem of his tweed waistcoat. "You have too much potential to throw away just because you're enrolled in the wrong degree. Can I borrow your pen for a moment?"

Amari handed it over and he pulled her notepad closer and wrote something at the top of the page. He returned the pen and then put his finger to his lips. "This is our little secret," he whispered, winking. Then he touched the edge of his tweed flat cap before strolling off.

Amari hesitated. She'd been warned since childhood to steer clear of men who wanted to keep secrets. But she'd known Professor Bottenfeldt for a while now. He was eccentric, no denying that, but she trusted him.

Her fingers twitched as her curiosity piqued. She pulled the paper closer.

She frowned as she read the single sentence. *"Seek Illumination amongst the bat willows."*

She didn't know what it meant, or why that one word had been capitalised. But she was going to find out.

⋇⋇⋇

The wind tousled Amari's curls as she marched along Addison's Walk, the susurration of the trees along the path sounding eerie in the dark. She had her mobile's flashlight on, a tiny pinpoint of light in the blackness of the woods.

A small cry escaped her lips as something suddenly darted in front of her. Amari flashed the light towards the movement and bit her lower lip to prevent from screaming. A deer barred her way. Or what used to be a deer. It was monstrously misshapen, its body bulging with bony growths that jutted unnaturally through its hairless hide. Purple veins stood out across its rump and its red eyes glared at her from underneath scythe-like antlers protruding from its forehead, where a small patch of diamond-shaped fur glinted in the torchlight. Amari tasted bile in her throat. It was the little fawn Doctor Clarke had had her eyes on.

It pawed the ground as it scowled at her. Then it bleated, a sound Amari would shudder at until her dying day.

She turned and ran.

Branches snapped at her face as she ploughed past the trees and into the field on the other side, where a pale sliver of moon overhead shed just enough light to see by. She risked a glance across her shoulder and wished she hadn't. The monster was right behind her, its head lowered and its antlers ready to spear her. Fear spurted adrenaline into her limbs. She had never run so fast in her life before.

Suddenly, her foot tripped over something, and she tumbled to the ground. She threw her arms over her head and felt grit and gravel bounce off them as the deer barrelled right past her. She looked up to see it scrambling as it turned to face her again.

Lying flat on her stomach, Amari's heart lurched into her throat. She was going to die here, in this field, in this foreign land, without having done anything yet. She hadn't even finished her bloody paper.

The beast stampeded towards her, antlers lowered.

Amari didn't think, she just shouted. The whispered word she had learned from the flickering lights underneath the Bridge of Sighs exploded from her lips. The earth before her ruptured open. Amari scrabbled away as the monstrous deer fell into the chasm, its dreadful screech coming suddenly to an abrupt end.

Gasping for breath, Amari struggled to her feet. Her whole body shook as she inched towards the rift in the earth. She peered into it. The broken body of the grotesque creature lay at the bottom, unmoving.

Tears pooled at the corners of her eyes, and she swallowed back a sob. She hadn't meant to kill it. She'd only wanted to escape.

What was this strange power she'd discovered? How did she suddenly live in a world where monsters and unicorns and magic words were real? It was ugly, and she wanted no part of it. She wanted – no, *needed*! – to be away from this place.

Vision blurred by the tears now streaming freely down her face, Amari started running. She ran as if she were still being chased, until the wind stung her face, until her breath was ragged. Until there were trees all around her and the moon was obscured again. Until the hurt in her chest was a different kind of pain.

Amari stumbled to a halt, heart hammering as she looked around. Trees surrounded her, only faintly darker outlines against the pitch blackness of the night. One tree she recognised, its symmetrical shape a clear sign it was manmade. The Wallinger sculpture. She was in Bat Willow Meadow.

An electronic beep shattered the silence and Amari nearly leapt into the air, her hands shaking as she pulled her mobile phone out again. The battery was on five percent. The clock said just after nine.

Trembling, Amari stood in the dark, listening for something, anything, to give her a clue why Professor Bottenfeldt had sent her here. His message had said to search for illumination, and she knew he'd meant it metaphorically, but she wouldn't mind a bit of actual light right now. She'd never liked the dark much.

How long she stood there, too afraid to move, Amari couldn't tell. A minute, maybe five. Maybe an hour. And then… She blinked. Was that a light over there? Goosebumps broke out on Amari's arms as a dozen glimmering sparks suddenly flickered to life around her.

Enthralled, Amari watched the lights slowly floating towards her. They were not the same as the ones that had whispered strange words underneath the Bridge of Sighs. Instead, these lights glowed a pale blue and a strange humming sound echoed around the meadow, almost like the noise a seashell makes when you hold it to your ear.

Amari had read about will-o'-wisps during her folklore studies, and she knew enough not to follow them, but these lights weren't trying to lure her anywhere. Instead, they seemed to be drawn to her. They were so close she could almost touch them as they swirled languidly around her.

"Illumination," Amari breathed, mesmerised, and stuck her finger out towards the blue spark floating past her.

The moment she touched it, the light exploded into rainbow colours, and all the other sparks around her shattered too, wrapping Amari in what she imagined the aurora borealis must look like. Dazzling colours swirled dizzyingly around her. As she gaped at the lights, their soft humming surged into a symphony that drowned out all Amari's thoughts, all her fears. Her entire body thrummed with vibrant, creative energy. She wanted to dance. She wanted to sing. She wanted to write!

Amari gasped as the thesis statement for her

paper suddenly popped into her head, and her hands shook as she realised she knew exactly what she was going to write. "Illumination!" she shouted jubilantly into the night.

Then the symphony dwindled, the rainbow colours faded. Amari was left in the dark, her panting breaths the only noise, feeling as if her supply of oxygen had suddenly been cut off.

Fear shot through Amari's heart like ice. What if this inspiration only lasted as long as the light?

Pulling her mobile from her pocket, she turned the flashlight on again, and then sprinted for the library.

⁂⁂⁂

Amari's eyes were burning as she dropped her pen on the table and slumped back in her chair. It was done. She'd done it. She glanced at her mobile. It was ten minutes to midnight.

She jumped up, hastily grabbing her things, and dashed into the printing room. Nervously, she watched the ticking hands of the clock on the wall as she waited for the old desktop PC to boot up and the scanner to flash into life.

Her hands shook as she scanned her handwritten papers into a PDF and then uploaded the document to the submission page. Sweat formed at the base of her neck as the progress bar stuck on 99%. Amari glanced at the clock again – she had seconds left. And then – success! – her paper was uploaded, and she punched the submit button just before midnight struck.

Amari's knees wobbled as she stumbled out of the library. She took a deep breath, letting the cool night air wash over her. Her shoulders relaxed. So, this was what freedom felt like.

Her mobile buzzed in her back pocket. Amari

was tempted to ignore it. She'd never felt so tired before in her life. Inspiration had come and gone and left her utterly exhausted. All she wanted to do was fall into bed and sleep for three days.

Reluctantly, she pulled the phone out. The screen lit up with an incoming text. Amari stopped dead in her tracks.

-- Only static around the labs right now. Thought you'd want to know. --

The phoned died in her hands as Amari stared at it.

Static could only mean one thing. The unicorn was back.

Amari broke into a sprint.

※※※

Sure enough, the campus gate stood open when Amari, gasping for breath, stumbled into the Science Area. The black van was parked next to the back entry to the labs, just like the previous times. Amari tried the door. It opened easily, and she heard a ruckus coming from down the hallway.

Ignoring the squeaking of her sneakers on the laminate floor, Amari dashed towards the light shining through the window in the door at the end of the corridor. Doctor Clarke's lab. A whinny sounded, and Amari quickened her pace.

Without thinking, she flung open the lab door and stormed in. Her sneakers protested again as she came to an abrupt halt.

Fluorescent light sparkled on the unicorn's mane, like stars in a silken sky. The creature was rearing on its hind legs, kicking its snowy white hooves into the air. Doctor Clarke, dressed in a white lab coat and wearing blue latex gloves, jumped backwards just in time. "Get that animal under control!" she shouted.

Off to one side, Amari noticed Dawson bent over and gasping for breath, as if he'd had the wind knocked out of him. A man Amari hadn't seen before, but who looked like an older version of the lanky pet shop owner, stepped in front of the unicorn, his hands raised placatingly.

"Come now, Una darling, this is for science," the man cajoled, slowly moving closer to the animal.

The unicorn – Una – rolled her eyes as she backed away. Her hindquarters pushed up against a wall and she squealed, baring her teeth at the man. He took a step towards her.

From the corner of her eye, Amari saw Doctor Clarke also sidling closer. In one hand, she held a long-needled syringe filled with what looked like molten quicksilver. Amari's heart lurched into her throat. The serum! Doctor Clarke wasn't going to draw the unicorn's blood – she was going to inject the creature with the serum!

A vision of the monstrous deer that had tried to spear her earlier that night flashed before Amari's eyes. With a scream, she threw herself at Doctor Clarke, pushing the woman off her feet. The syringe clattered to the floor.

"Stop this!" she shouted, thrusting herself between the older man and the unicorn, heedless of the animal's silver horn at her back. "You can't let her do this! She's not some lab mouse to experiment on! Look at her!"

Amari could feel the unicorn's warm breath on her neck. She turned slightly, letting the sweet scent of apples and magic waft over her as the creature nuzzled closer. Her hand found the velvety coat and goosebumps erupted across her arms. "Just look at her," she breathed, awestruck.

"I have looked," Doctor Clarke sneered, climbing to her feet. "And all I see is potential." She lunged towards the unicorn, the syringe aloft, her eyes gleaming with something that frightened Amari to her core.

Amari reacted instinctively. She jumped into Doctor Clarke's path, crying out in pain as the needle stabbed into her chest and a rush of warmth flooded her body as the serum spread through her veins. Her knees wobbled and she stumbled to the floor. Doctor Clarke's horrified expression was the last thing she saw clearly as her vision fogged.

She thought she saw the room erupt in a searing white light. Una screamed again, and then someone grunted – through the haze it looked like the unicorn's horn was protruding from the unknown man's back. Amari's limbs were like jelly as she tried to get up. She heard glass shattering and many voices shouting. A table upended next to her, and she tried to crawl away, but her body sunk to the floor, too heavy to lift. She blinked, but everything seemed to happen in slow motion.

Pain exploded across her forehead and suddenly all Amari could think of was the deer she had seen earlier that night, its scythe-like horns slicing at her. Was she going to turn into a monster, too?

With the last bit of her fading strength, Amari pulled the small vial of purplish liquid she had found at the pet shop from her jacket pocket. The thought of drinking Una's blood sent a spasm of nausea through her, but it was her only chance. With numb fingers, she fumbled with the stopper. The vial slipped from her hand and shattered on the floor.

Amari let her head drop to the cold ground. Through the fog, she could just see a line of purple fluid pooling out of reach.

"Miss Kerubo?" She thought she heard Professor Bottenfeldt's voice through the surrounding chaos.

Amari blinked again, sluggishly turning her head towards the sound. Fire seared through her veins, but she was too weak to scream. Her chest felt heavy. Every breath was agony.

"Hold on, Amari." Professor Bottenfeldt's voice again. "You're going to be alright."

And then the world turned white.

⋇⋇⋇

Voices whispered forgotten words in the darkness. Amari whirled around. Trees, everywhere. Rainbows danced across the sky. Waves of colour washed over her, threatening to drown her. A face floated into view. Her mother's. "Make us proud." Amari slapped her hands across her ears as the words echoed in her head, growing louder and louder. A monstrous deer jumped at her, stabbing at her with grotesquely twisted horns. Pain blossomed in her chest, searingly hot. Then, suddenly, nothing. All was dark. All was quiet.

Amari opened her eyes. She was lying in a four-poster bed in a room with tapestries on the walls but no windows. She could hear nothing but her own heartbeat drumming in her ears. Her mouth felt tacky, like she hadn't had anything to drink in days. Her eyelids were heavy.

She closed her eyes, just for a moment, and when she woke up again, she was in a sterile white room, a tube sticking out of her arm and the steady beat of a heart rate monitor beeping beside her.

Amari pushed herself up into a sitting position and looked around. She was in a small room with a window in one wall through which she could see nurses hurrying past. A table in one corner groaned underneath the weight of an enormous bunch of proteas in a glass vase. Above it, a helium balloon with the words Get Better Soon printed in happy colours bobbed merrily.

A hospital.

The sound of someone clearing his throat startled her and she looked up to see Professor Harris standing in the doorway, awkwardly holding a small bouquet of white carnations. "May I come in?" he asked.

Amari suppressed a sigh. The last thing she wanted was another lecture on how her actions reflected upon the university, but she nodded, and Professor Harris placed the flowers on the table before pulling a chair closer to her bedside.

"How are you feeling?"

"Like I've been trampled by a herd of wildebeest," she replied truthfully.

Her student advisor stared blankly at her for a moment, no doubt trying to conjure the foreign image in his mind's eye, before he took a handkerchief out of his pocket and started cleaning his glasses. The silence stretched awkwardly as Amari waited for him to finish.

Finally, he put his glasses back on and looked at her. "The university regrets the incident," he said, shuffling uncomfortably in his seat. "And we hope this token of goodwill will help towards making some amends for your suffering." He pulled an envelope out of his pocket and handed it to her.

Amari took it, staring at the university's logo imprinted on the expensive paper.

"This… incident," she said, hesitant to open the letter. "How did I get here?"

"Professor Bottenfeldt called an ambulance. It

was fortunate that he'd had a restless night and happened upon the scene. Rest assured, Doctor Clarke is no longer a member of faculty and will face the full consequences of the law."

"Okay…" Amari replied, trying to mask her confusion. Was the unicorn's presence in the lab common knowledge now? If so, her sceptical philosophy lecturer was handling the news remarkably well. "And she'll be prosecuted for…?"

"For experimenting with hazardous toxins and endangering students in the process," Professor Harris exclaimed, a flush of anger heating his cheeks. "I hope you'll consider testifying against her when the time comes."

Amari stared at the man. He only knew half of the story. She should have expected as much, but why hadn't Professor Bottenfeldt told him the whole truth?

"The doctor says your recovery was remarkable," Professor Harris said. "He doesn't expect any side effects from the… poisoning." He coughed, embarrassed.

Amari looked at the envelope again, suddenly burning to know what the university deemed appropriate recompense for nearly getting killed by your research supervisor. She tore it open and pulled out a document printed on the university's official letterhead. Her eyes widened as she scanned the contents. They were offering her a full scholarship for her postgraduate studies!

Startled, she gaped at Professor Harris. "But…? I…" she stuttered, flustered. "I don't deserve this!"

"Oh, come now, Miss Kerubo, give yourself some credit. That final essay you handed in was inspired. A stroke of genius, some might even say." The professor fiddled with one of the buttons on his coat. Amari noticed a loose thread hanging from it. "I must admit, I had my doubts, but you've proven me wrong. I look forward to seeing what more you might bring to the table."

Amari folded the letter up, suddenly embarrassed. "I'll… think about it."

Professor Harris rose to his feet. "I'll leave you to your rest. Please don't hesitate to call me if you need anything. The university will assist wherever we can. I know it must be difficult for you, on your own, in a foreign country."

Amari quirked an eyebrow. "Thank you," she said, trying not to let cynicism cloud her voice. They'd never cared all that much about her before. They were probably scared witless she'd run to the papers or take them to court. A bursary was an easy way to assure her goodwill.

Professor Harris left the room, and Amari lay back down again, her thoughts spinning. Her family would be proud, but she knew in her heart that academics was no longer the path for her. How could she lock herself up, grappling with long-dead thinkers, when she knew unicorns existed?

That Davids fellow might not be so delusional after all…

Amari scoffed at the thought.

A jaunty tune suddenly filled the room and it took her a moment to recognise her mobile's ring tone. She found it vibrating in the drawer of a side table. Her mother's face filled the screen.

"Mama?" she answered.

Her mother's relief was palpable, even though they were a world apart. "Amari! I hope I'm not waking you up. How do you feel?"

"I'm fine, Mama. Just a little tired."

"What happened? That professor with the German name called. He said you'd been in an accident?"

Amari suppressed a sigh. She appreciated Professor Bottenfeldt's thoughtfulness, but it would have been easier if her mother hadn't known. "Just a little accident in the lab. The doctor said I'll be fine."

"The lab! Amari, your degree is in politics! What were you doing in a lab?"

And there it was.

Amari took a deep breath. "Mama, I don't want to be in politics. I hate it." She braced herself for her mother's reaction.

After a brief pause, her mother's voice was quiet on the other end of the line. "Why didn't you tell me?"

"I… I was afraid to disappoint you." She swallowed back a sudden lump in her throat.

"Hai wena!" her mother exclaimed. "You can never disappoint me, Amari. If you don't want to do politics, then don't. I only want you to be happy. It's your life and only you can decide what matters most to you. Whatever you choose, I will always be proud of you."

Amari laughed even as tears streamed down her cheeks. "You're not mad?"

"I'm not mad," her mother said, the smile audible in her voice. "Now, promise me you'll be more careful next time. And you'll come home for a visit soon."

"I promise."

The battery on Amari's phone was beeping again by the time she ended the call, feeling like a weight had been lifted from her shoulders. She should have come clean months ago.

Now all she had to do was figure out what she wanted to do with her life.

She may never know what had happened to Una the unicorn, but there were plenty of other, less exotic, animals out there that needed her help. She might look Tristan up and see if she could join his organisation. They'd know what she could do.

Of one thing Amari was sure. She'd found her focus, and she was going to chase it down with all her heart.

⁂

It was a beautiful day. There was hardly a cloud in the sky and the deer were frolicking in the Grove next to Magdalen College's grounds. Amari stood by the fence, her suitcase on the ground by her feet, gazing wistfully at the animals. She was going to miss them.

Inside her jacket pocket, her hand gripped the letter she had received from the Zoological Society of London a few days ago. Her zoology marks had drawn their attention and they'd offered her a position as junior zookeeper. She'd accepted immediately.

Her mobile pinged and she looked at the display. Her taxi was here. She'd better go or she'd miss her train.

"Going somewhere, Miss Kerubo? I hope it's not too far away."

Amari turned to see Professor Bottenfeldt ambling towards her. She hadn't seen the Emeritus Professor since that night at the lab, and no matter how many times she'd gone by his office or waited for him at the library, he'd proven strangely elusive.

"Far enough," she replied. She wasn't quite ready to return home just yet – after all, there was still an entire world to explore – but she was more than willing to leave Oxford behind.

She hesitated. Professor Bottenfeldt's smile was as open and friendly as ever. But how do you broach the subject of a unicorn?

A spark of humour twinkled in the old man's eyes. "You've decided not to take the university up on its generous offer, then?"

Amari shook her head.

"Then I'm glad I found you in time. I have an alternative proposition for you."

Amari lifted an enquiring eyebrow and the Professor chuckled. "I've been following your career at Oxford for some time, Miss Kerubo, and I'm not ashamed to say that I had a look at your latest academic record. We both know you wasted your time pursuing politics, my dear Amari. But you excelled at your extracurricular subjects: zoology, mythology, botany, classical studies… You have all the hallmarks of the candidate I'm looking for."

Amari frowned. "Candidate for what, exactly?"

Professor Bottenfeldt coughed. "My dear, let's address the unicorn in the room."

Amari gaped at him.

"And the glimmerlings that helped inspire that magnificent final paper you handed in. And I'm fairly sure you've also encountered their cousins, the luminaires, at some point, otherwise how would you explain your uncanny knack for opening locked doors?" He winked at her as she gasped. "Yes, I have looked at the CCTV footage, but unlike your talented friend in IT, I know how to recognise magic at work."

"You know… about *all* of it?"

"Indeed, Miss Kerubo. And if you'll follow me down the rabbit hole, I can show you so much more. There is a world hidden right underneath everyone's noses – one you've just touched the edges of as yet. Would you like to go deeper?"

A flush of adrenaline tingled through her body. A world of magic. A world where unicorns exist and rainbows whisper inspiration in your ears… Goosebumps lifted on her arms.

Her mobile pinged again, and she blinked, disorientated. Her attention returned to Professor Bottenfeldt. He raised his eyebrows in a questioning gaze.

Amari looked at her phone. She was definitely going to miss her train. She turned it on silent.

"Show me," she said.

Professor Bottenfeldt smiled, and then the world turned white.

※※※

When she could see again, Amari stood before two enormous steel gates embedded in the side of a mountain. She looked behind her to see a narrow footpath leading down a steep slope towards a little village in the distance surrounded by snowcapped mountain peaks.

Amari gulped. At a guess, she'd say they were somewhere in the Alps right now. Wherever they were, it certainly wasn't in Oxford anymore. And they had travelled there within the blink of an eye.

"Where are we?" she asked, shivering as an icy breeze tugged at the scarf around her neck.

Professor Bottenfeldt didn't answer as he walked towards the gates. He said a word, his mouth almost caressing the strange sound, and Amari gasped as she recognised it as the one she had learned from the… what had he called the lights underneath the bridge? Luminaires?

The doors swung open and Professor Bottenfeldt turned and winked at her.

"Welcome to the Repository," he said.

Amari stared at the tunnel on the other side of the gates. Its sides looked like they had been carved from the rock itself, smooth and sheer. Lights suspended from the ceiling every few feet trailed off into the distance. Amari hesitated.

"You will not be disappointed," Professor Bottenfeldt nudged gently.

Amari gritted her teeth and nodded. She stepped into the mountain. The great doors clanged shut behind her.

"Follow me," Professor Bottenfeldt said as he strode quickly down the corridor.

Amari hurried to keep up with him, afraid to get lost as they moved deeper into the mountain, past many other corridors and doors, until they finally reached a steel door at the end of a hallway. The professor paused at the door.

"After you."

Amari raised an eyebrow, but the man merely nodded encouragingly. Her hand lingered on the cold door handle. She had a feeling that, no matter what lay on the other side of that door, her life would never be the same again after this. She took a deep breath. Then she opened the door and stepped out onto a steel platform.

Goosebumps erupted all over her body.

Before her lay a huge cavern filled with enclosures, like one might see at a zoo. The air was thick with the cacophony of many clamouring voices. Her gaze drifted from pen to pen, amazed at what she saw. From inside one enclosure, a muscular one-eyed monster stared dumbly back at her as it sat chewing on what looked like a roasted sheep. In another, a bull-headed man – a minotaur! – scribbled on the walls of a maze that disappeared out of view. Further on, a group of women were busy having tea next to the banks of a river beside a woodland area. Everywhere Amari looked, something more unbelievable caught her attention.

"What is this place?" she breathed.

Beside her, Professor Bottenfeldt's answer was

muted, his voice tinged with awe too. "We call it the Repository. The last stronghold for creatures of myth. We house them here to protect them from the outside world."

Amari's gaze snapped towards the professor's. "We?"

"The Council for the Protection and Preservation of Cultural Creatures, or CPPCC for short." He laughed at her incredulous look. "Quite a mouthful, I know. In the mythical world, we're more commonly known as the Elder Council. For centuries, we've gathered mythical creatures here, where they can exist in safety without being subjected to exploitation or being hunted to extinction."

"But… why?" Amari looked out across the cavern. They were all real. She could hardly believe it.

"Why protect them? Because the world needs them, Amari. Come, walk with me." He led her down the steel steps and, as they walked past the tall walls of the unmarked enclosures, Professor Bottenfeldt's tone turned serious. "You know why Doctor Clarke wanted the unicorn, don't you?"

Amari nodded. She vividly remembered the miraculous way in which the damaged cells in the petri dish had regenerated when they encountered the sample blood. "Because unicorn blood can cure any disease."

Professor Bottenfeldt pursed his lips into a thin line. "Can you imagine what would happen to the unicorn if the world found out about that?"

Amari shuddered. Una would know nothing but needles and experiments. She would be prodded and poked and cut and sliced by blue latex-covered hands until they went too far and she'd end up a trophy on someone's wall.

"In here," Professor Bottenfeldt said as he

opened one of the enclosure doors. Amari stepped into a wooded grove, bathed in twilight. Fireflies danced in air thick with the scent of night-blooming lilies. Somewhere out of a sight, a small brook murmured softly.

"What the world doesn't know is that we cannot endanger these mythical creatures," Professor Bottenfeldt said softly beside her as he led her through the trees towards a small clearing. "Each creature is associated with a trait, and if we lose the creature, the world will lose that trait. Do you know what trait a unicorn protects?"

Amari had read enough classical literature to guess at the answer. "Purity," she replied.

The professor nodded. "There is only one unicorn left in the world, and we are her guardians."

Amari's breath hitched in her throat as the unicorn trotted into the clearing. Her silky coat shone in the moonlight, and her spiralled horn glimmered with pearlescent hues as the light caught it. The creature trotted closer and Amari inhaled deeply as it stopped a hand's breadth away from her, letting its magical scent waft over her. Amari ached to touch her, her hand hovering just above the unicorn's nose.

"Una's last guardian betrayed her," Professor Bottenfeldt said, his voice bitter with resentment. "And he paid the ultimate price for it."

Vaguely, Amari remembered a horn protruding from a man's back. Dawson. Or Dawson Senior, the lanky man's father. Her memories of that night were still foggy.

"But *you* won't."

Starled, Amari turned towards the professor. His smile was both fatherly and proud.

"Amari Kerubo, will you join us? Will you become the Keeper of Exotic Animals?"

The unicorn pushed her head forward and into Amari's hand. She stroked its soft coat and inhaled the creature's sweet scent, feeling all her fears fade. Una nickered softly, and Amari knew.

She had finally found her calling. She would be the Keeper of Exotic Animals.

"I will," she said as the unicorn nuzzled at her fingertips.

Bonus Flash Fiction

Bottenfeldt's Disappointment

It was a lovely night in Oxford, and Professor Bottenfeldt tucked his thumbs into the pockets of his tweed waistcoat as he ambled past old Gothic university buildings on his way back to his flat. After spending the evening at a charity event listening to Wagner and fondly reminiscing about the country he'd left behind so many years ago, he'd felt magnanimous and had made a sizeable donation towards a fund aimed at preserving the last few members of the Black Forest wolf pack. Much as he loved his adopted city, he did sometimes miss the mountains and forests of Bavaria.

He turned into a small side street and jarred to a halt as the flashing blue lights of a police car and a crowd of onlookers blocked his way. Bottenfeldt's gaze drifted towards the sign above the shop that seemed to be the focus of attention - *Dawson & Son's Exotic Pet Emporium.*

The professor tutted. He'd made it his life's purpose to protect exotic animals, and here was someone selling them as pets.

He wondered what had drawn the police here tonight. Perhaps they'd found something illegal being sold in the shop? Curious, he drew closer to the commotion.

"Damn kids," he heard someone growl. "Everything's a joke to them."

Bottenfeldt peered over a bystander's shoulder to see a policeman usher three young people out of the pet shop and into the back of the car. His lips pressed into a thin line as he recognised the last one – Amari Kerubo, one of his favourite students. Her interest in mythology and ancient lore almost equalled his own. He would have expected to find her in a quiet recess of the library, surrounded by piles of ancient tomes, not in the back of a police car with her hands in cuffs. Her dark eyes widened as she spotted him in the crowd just before she climbed into the car.

"What happened here?" Bottenfeldt asked the woman standing next to him.

He felt something bump into his leg and looked down just in time to see a chinchilla scurry off into the alley.

"Looks like they pranked the pet shop," the woman responded. "Broke in and set all the animals free. Can't say I blame them. Poor things, locked up like that."

Bottenfeldt frowned. He wouldn't have taken Miss Kerubo for the type to play pranks, especially those that amounted to theft, and got the police involved. And while he was all for setting the poor animals loose, what would become of them now? That chinchilla might be free now, but odds are it would end up in a cat's belly by dawn. What good would its freedom be then?

Foolishness. Utter foolishness.

No, this 'prank' was ill-considered and an unnecessary risk of her academic career. She'd be lucky if the pet shop owner didn't press any charges and if he did, the university would have to take steps to protect its reputation. At best, she'd have to spend the night in a jail cell – and it might just do her good to reflect upon the consequences of this imprudent escapade.

He'd expected more from her. He'd even been thinking of grooming her as a Keeper's apprentice, a role that would suit her talents much better than her chosen study path. But how could he trust her with *that* kind of responsibility if she didn't consider the consequences of her actions?

It was a shame, really.

Disappointment tasted bitter in Bottenfeldt's mouth as he resumed his journey home, all the while shaking his head in bitter frustration.

In Need of a Fishbowl

The previous night's incident still plagued Bottenfeldt the next morning as he retraced his steps and found himself walking past the pet shop again. A sleepless night had convinced him that there must have been more to Miss Kerubo's actions than a mere lark. He'd known her for almost three years now, and she just wasn't the type. She must have had a good reason to break into the pet shop…

He glanced at his watch. He was due to present at a small symposium within an hour, but that gave him enough time to satisfy his curiosity.

An overpowering smell of disinfectant assailed his nose as he entered the shop. The owner – Dawson presumably – was on his knees scrubbing the floor underneath an empty cage. He grimaced as he climbed to his feet, his knuckles white around a grubby scrubbing brush. He was a long-limbed man with gaunt features that Bottenfeldt found vaguely familiar.

"What can I help you with?" Dawson asked irritably. "Unless you're after a fish, I'm afraid you'll have to wait until I've got new stock in."

Bottenfeldt's gaze swept across the empty shop. The man was right. Apart from the undisturbed fish tanks, every cage in the shop was empty. Amari and her friends had been thorough.

"I heard about the commotion last night. Any idea why the kids would do this?"

Dawson glowered. "Self-righteous tree-huggers, no doubt. Think the world would be a better place if we all went vegan. What's next? Giving animals the vote?" He tossed the brush into a bucket of dirty water and winced as water splashed across his trousers.

Bottenfeldt sensed Dawson's mood would not be improved by mentioning that he was vegan himself.

"What'll it be then? Guppy? Goldfish? Or maybe something more *exotic*?"

Bottenfeldt's eyes narrowed at the inflection on the last word. Something in the man's tone made the professor wonder if Dawson wasn't awaiting his response just a little too keenly. The question lingered in the air between them.

"Exotic?" the professor finally ventured. Did he imagine the flash of disappointment in the man's eyes, before his face smoothed into neutrality?

"This way," Dawson said, turning on his heals and leading Bottenfeldt to a tank containing a single, sapphire fish with large flowing fins gracefully circling its container.

"Siamese fighting fish," Dawson explained. "Only have the one left – it killed all the others that were in here with it. Could win you a decent amount of quid, if you're the betting kind."

Bottenfeldt clenched his fists. This was exactly the type of thing he'd been campaigning against all his life! For a brief moment, he wished he'd been here with Amari last night, liberating whatever this man had been willing to sell to unscrupulous buyers. He fought down his outrage, his eyes darting towards the back of the shop as he tried to control his expression.

The blinking light of a security camera drew his attention. Strangely, it wasn't pointing at the shop, or even towards the till, but was positioned to keep watch on a door in the back wall.

"Do you have more stock behind that door?" he asked. If the man was holding anything illegal, it would probably be hidden out of sight.

Dawson glanced at the door and shrugged. "No, nothing special there. Just my office. Look, do you want the fish or not?" His chin jutted out belligerently, as if his patience had been exhausted.

"Yes, of course."

The man caught and transferred the fish into a little plastic bag with such alacrity he must have been afraid Bottenfeldt would change his mind. As it was, the professor winced as he handed his credit card over to pay the fish's exorbitant price.

As he waited for the transaction to go through, Bottenfeldt scanned the shelves behind the counter, which contained an assortment of paraphernalia ranging from ointments to pet vitamins. The smell of disinfectant was less pronounced here. Instead, a strange scent seemed to linger in the air. Almost like the smell of burnt tea leaves.

"Declined," the pet shop owner said, not bothering to hide the look of annoyance on his face.

"Terribly sorry." Bottenfeldt rummaged through the pockets of his wallet, trying to ignore the lanky man's disapproving stare. "Try this one instead."

He breathed a relieved sigh as, this time, the

transaction went through. He made a mental note to review his budget before the next worthy cause found him short.

A few seconds later, Bottenfeldt stepped out of the pet shop, plastic bag in hand, and squinted down at the fish. "Well, old chap," he muttered. "What am I going to do with you now? Couldn't just leave you there, could I?" The fish, predictably, didn't respond.

It occurred to him then that he probably should have bought a fishbowl as well.

He glanced at his watch. He was going to be late!

As he hurried across the street, Bottenfeldt noticed another CCTV camera mounted on the wall and pointing towards the pet shop. With his free hand, he scratched at his beard. Something about this place just didn't feel right.

But he didn't have time to ponder the matter now. He had a presentation to deliver.

A Flag to Capture

Phumlani winced as the doorhandle slipped out of his grasp and slammed shut, the sound reverberating through the vast emptiness of the cathedral. Gripping his laptop closer to his chest, he tiptoed down the nave towards his usual spot. It was close to midnight and only a few scattered lights burned dimly in secluded corners, barely enough for him to see by. He bit back a curse as he stubbed his toe against the solid wood of a pew.

If he hadn't been looking forward to this raid for weeks already, he'd be fast asleep in a warm bed right now. Unfortunately, most of his squad were based in the US, so he was going to have to red-eye his way through it. And since the Wi-Fi in his dorm room could never keep up with the lag produced by twenty squads of six gamers each fighting it out on one enormous map, he had no choice but to sneak in here at the dead of night.

Clutching onto a carved post, he took a moment for his eyes to adjust to the darkness. Eerie shadows filled the cathedral, and although he was not superstitious – apart from a healthy respect for the tokoloshe that his *gogo* had instilled in him at an early age – his heart still lurched into his throat as the darkness shifted to reveal a figure emerging from one of the shadowy alcoves.

Phumlani expelled a breath as the light revealed a silver-haired man in a three-piece tweed suit. Relief and recognition dawned at the same moment as Phumlani realised he was looking at Amari's old mythology professor, the one with the strange German surname.

"Don't mind me, Mr Mahlangu," the professor said in a thick accent, a hint of a smile playing at his lips. "I'm sure you have an important flag to capture."

Phumlani gasped. "How did you…?"

The professor pointed up towards the soaring Gothic arches above. "There's always someone watching."

Phumlani squinted upwards in the faint light. Had they installed security cameras in the church? But no, all he could make out were the cathedral's gargoyles staring sightlessly back at him. The old man must be slightly sun-touched. Although that was highly unlikely, given their current location. Maybe he was referring to God?

Shrugging, Phumlani dropped into his seat and flipped his laptop open. A window popped up on the screen – the feed from the security camera Amari had asked him to monitor. He'd been monitoring it on and off during the day, but the basement in the picture had remained stubbornly, boringly, empty.

"What's that?" the professor asked.

Frantically, Phumlani tapped at the laptop's touchpad in search of his mouse pointer, but not before the old man had taken a step closer.

"Don't tell me you've hacked into someone's security feed, Mr Mahlangu."

"I… oh, um…" Phumlani stammered. "It's nothing. Nothing to worry about." He cleared his throat, embarrassed, as he felt the professor's watery blue eyes bore into him. "Just a basement. Really, it's nothing. It's in a pet shop," he finished lamely, as if that made everything okay.

The man's eyes narrowed and Phumlani chided himself for talking too much. He clamped his lips shut as he averted his eyes from the professor's disapproving stare. He hitched a breath as he saw what was happening to the feed.

"Not again!" he blurted before he could stop himself.

"What?" the old man asked sharply.

For a moment, Phumlani weighed his words. He could get himself, and Amari, into some serious trouble if the professor turned out to be an unreasonable man. But Amari had always spoken highly of him. Besides, the old man seemed to know more than he reasonably should already. Phumlani decided to trust him.

"This basement is always empty," he explained. "Nothing ever happens. Except some nights, around midnight, the feed just goes static for a few minutes. See?" He turned the laptop so the professor could get a better look.

The old man's face paled visibly. Phumlani hoped he wasn't having a heart attack or something.

The professor licked his lips, as if his throat had suddenly gone dry. "What happens when the static disappears?"

"Nothing…" Phumlani said, trying not to alarm the man even further. "It goes back to normal, and the basement is still empty." The professor breathed out a sigh of relief, and Phumlani cleared his throat guiltily. "But then the feed from the camera in the shop goes static, and after that the feed in the street is down for a minute or two. Then it's all back to normal."

The old man swore softly. And then he muttered

something that Phumlani couldn't quite make out... It sounded like *smell* and *fox fire*, but that didn't make much sense. The professor's gaze was intent when he looked at Phumlani again. "I suppose you don't know where the static travels to next, do you?"

"As a matter of fact, I do."

Phumlani tapped on the minimised windows at the bottom of the screen until he found the one he was looking for. A grainy picture of the outside of the biology labs appeared. "Now we just wait for the magic mist, and then the static comes."

"Magic mist?" The professor's lips pursed into a thin line. Phumlani winced as the old man urgently tapped his finger against the screen. "Where is this?"

"Science campus. The back of the biology labs."

The professor's eyes widened in alarm. "So *that's* what she was doing!" He spun on his heels and stormed down the nave. "Good work, Mr Mahlangu," he called over his shoulder. "Don't tell anyone about this!" The church door slammed behind him.

Phumlani stared after him for a few seconds, not sure if he was in trouble or not. He glanced up at the gargoyles above. They hadn't moved.

He pulled his mobile phone out and quickly sent Amari a message. Then he tucked the phone away and pressed his headphones into his ears.

He had an important flag to capture.

Better on Our Side

"Where is the young woman now?"

Professor Bottenfeldt turned towards the speaker seated at the end of the boardroom table. The Chairman was still a young man, but he'd shown an astute ability in managing the members of the Elder Council since he had accepted the position a few months ago. Bottenfeldt hoped that with him in charge, they'd be able to restore the Repository to the glory days his grandfather had told him stories about - back when the legendary Keeper Diana Hartmann had still overseen the mountain fortress. Under her supervision, the fortress had indeed been a refuge for mythical creatures. These days, it sometimes seemed more like a penitentiary – a place where creatures were locked up just because they had committed the crime of existing.

The Chairman cleared his throat, subtly returning Bottenfeldt's thoughts to the present.

"She's recovered enough from the effects of the serum to be stable. I've had her moved from her room in the Repository to a hospital in Oxford."

"She should be disposed of." Bottenfeldt's gaze snapped towards the speaker: Council-member Silvetti, a woman whose lined face had the permanently sour expression of someone whose *sauerkraut* had too much vinegar in it. "She knows too much."

Murmurs of agreement rose from an alarming number of other Councilmembers sitting around the table. A shiver ran down Bottenfeldt's spine. The Council had never outright condoned murder before. He had to divert their fears, and fast.

"It need not come to that," he said. "A simple draft of Mnemosynth should suffice, as it has always done in the past. But –" He held a finger up, drawing everyone's attention to him. "I've been keeping an eye on Miss Kerubo's career these last three years. Had her under my wing, so to speak. She's a remarkably astute student and has excelled in all the subjects that matter: mythology, zoology, geography, linguistics… I believe she would be the perfect candidate."

"Candidate for what, exactly?" Silvetti pursed her lips together, making her look like someone sucking on a particularly bitter prune.

Bottenfeldt tucked his thumbs into the pockets of his tweed waistcoat as he directed his gaze towards the Chairman again. "The new Keeper of Exotic Animals."

The chamber erupted into a cacophony as every Councilmember tried to shout at once.

"Betrayed by our own Keeper!"

"No one to teach her –"

"How can we trust –?"

"Who will take care of them now?"

The Chairman lifted both hands in a gesture of peace and the ruckus quickly died down.

"Filling the Keeper's position should be our paramount priority," he said in a tone that brooked no arguments. "The safety of the Repository's residents was entrusted to us – a duty we have all failed at by not uncovering these illicit activities sooner." Bottenfeldt felt the pang of guilt touch his own heart, and saw some Councilmembers drop their heads in shame. "And since both Keeper Blake and his son died during the incident, we will probably now never get to the bottom of their smuggling activities."

"Probably not," Bottenfeldt agreed. He was still amazed at how the deceased Keeper had kept his son, Dawson, hidden from the Council by the mere expedient of having different last names.

"But I will vouch for Miss Kerubo," he added. "We can trust her not to follow in her predecessor's footsteps. It was her actions taken against her supervisor's research activities that led me to discover Una's abuse. Without Amari's involvement, we could have lost the world's last unicorn in the name of science." He let that thought sink in before he continued. "Amari has proven herself to be resourceful, and I have reason to believe that she may already know a Word of Wonder."

A collective gasp rose around the table as Bottenfeldt told them about the chasm he had found – and closed again – on the way to Bat Willow Meadow. "I need not remind you that someone with this much untrained raw power could become quite formidable. I believe it would be better for all of us if Miss Kerubo was on our side."

The silence was palpable as the Elder Council considered his words.

Then another voice spoke up. "And what of the young man? The computer geek?"

Bottenfeldt turned towards Councilmember Mazzoni. The Italian man's slumped posture belied the keen interest in his eyes.

"He knows nothing," he said quickly, lest the topic of *silencing* was raised again. "But he's quite talented behind a keyboard. I've already passed his name onto my friends in MI6. You needn't worry about him. He'll be too occupied by national security to wonder about misbehaving CCTV feeds within pet shops."

Mazzoni nodded, seemingly satisfied, and Bottenfeldt waited patiently to see if anyone raised any other objections. When none came, he directed his attention back towards the head of the table.

"Then it's settled," the Chairman said, nodding at Bottenfeldt. "Extend our offer to Miss Kerubo, and let's hope she accepts. If she is half as capable as you think her to be, then we'd be lucky to have her."

"Very well," the professor said, allowing himself a pleased smile. "I will make all the necessary arrangements."

Councilmember Ramirez cleared her throat. She adjusted her glasses and peered at the stack of papers before her. "With that matter settled, let's move on to the next item on the agenda. There is still the matter of…"

Bottenfeldt allowed his mind to drift as the Council discussed less important matters. There was still much to do before Amari's arrival at the Repository. He had no doubt she would accept his offer. He had seen the way Una had reacted when Amari had been injured at the laboratory. The unicorn and the young woman shared a special bond – and that meant Amari was someone exceptional.

He could think of no one else he'd rather have as Keeper of Exotic Animals.

ACKNOWLEDGEMENTS

Writing a novel about a character's backstory is a tricky thing. Am I, as the author, merely indulging myself by thinking readers would be that interested in knowing where a specific character came from and why they are who they are? Since you've made it this far, I can now breathe a sigh of relief and say THANK YOU, dear reader, for caring enough to read this prequel and justifying my self-indulgence.

If you happen to be a member or alumni of Oxford University, please forgive me if Amari's experience didn't live up to your fond recollections. Personally, I would jump at the chance to study at such an esteemed institution and nothing negative I wrote in this story was meant to be taken as fact or seen as an indictment of this hallowed university, its students, or its faculty. I hope you don't mind that I took liberties while living vicariously through my character!

A HUGE thank you goes out to all the people in my life who support my writing! To Mari Terblanche and Thalia Fourie for beta reading, everyone on my ARC Team for spreading the word, my friends Claudette and Schalk for cheerleading, and my dad, Jannie, and husband, Gareth, for their non-stop encouragement and support. I could never do this without you!

WANT MORE?

Subscribe to Suneé le Roux's email list to receive a free and exclusive short story prequel set in the Mythical Menagerie universe, only available to newsletter subscribers!

SUBSCRIBE.SUNEELEROUX.COM/KEEPEROFEXOTICANIMALS

Please Review

If you've enjoyed this story, please consider leaving a review on your online platform of choice and/or on Goodreads. Think of it as word of mouth recommendation. Independent authors such as myself need reviews for visibility and social proof, and to get those algorithms to place my books in the hands of other readers.

It doesn't have to be a long and in-depth review - one sentence, or even just a star rating, will do.

It would mean the world to me. Thank you!

About the Author

Suneé le Roux is a whimsical wordsmith who crafts realistic worlds filled with hidden magic, drawing inspiration from her passion for travel and the mythical realms she has (disappointingly) only found in books (as yet!).

By day she toils in the IT industry, but at night she dreams of dragons and writes stories that aim to infuse the mundane with a little magic.

When not penning her next captivating adventure, Suneé finds inspiration in fantasy-based PC games (casting spells as a formidable enchantress) and geeky movie marathons, while fuelling her imaginative endeavours with copious amounts of chocolate.

She lives in South Africa with her husband and a young wizard-in-training.

She loves nothing more than to hear from readers. Connect with her here:

Website: www.suneeleroux.com

Email: contact@suneeleroux.com

Facebook: www.facebook.com/authorsuneeleroux/

Instagram: www.instagram.com/suneeleroux/

www.ingramcontent.com/pod-product-compliance
Lightning Source LLC
LaVergne TN
LVHW010627100826
845148LV00014B/3139

* 9 7 8 0 7 9 6 1 3 5 2 2 3 *